BEYOND THE BATTLEFIELD

A compilation of short stories and poems

Copyright © 2023

All rights reserved.

ISBN:9798863712772

All rights reserved, including the right to reproduce this book, or any portion thereof in any form. No part of this book may be reproduced, transmitted, downloaded, reverse engineered, or stored, in any form or introduced into any information storage and retrieval system, in any form or by any means, whither electronic or mechanical without the express written permission of the author.

CONTENTS

Page 1. A Growing Doubt
    by Maureen Myant.

Page 7. Tiny Pin Cushion Wumin
    by Greg Shearer.

Page 8. Writer's Retreat
    by Carolyn Mandache

Page 18. Prospecthill Road
    by Kathryn Metcalfe.

Page 19. The Sane Scientist's New Invention
    by Jane Jay Morrison.

Page 21. All Inclusive
    by Colette Coen.

Page 26. Padraig – Who Drove the Snakes Out of Ireland
    by Pratibha Castle.

Page 28. Rags to Rags in Three Generations
    by Frank Chambers.

Page 38. Handyman
    by Palma McKeown.

Page 40. Kissing Bridges
    by Barney MacFarlane.

Page 54. Laundry Lady
    by Marco Giannasi.

Page 56. London for a Tenner: 1980
    by Alex Meikle.

Page 63. Homework
    by Lizzie Allan.

Page 65. Heller's Lift
    by Ian Goudie.

Page 75. Love and Wisdom
    by Henry Buchanan.

Page 76. Area Z
    by Duncan McDonald.

Page 90. Partition
                                    by Yasmin Hanif.
Page 92. Reflections on Autism
                                    by Megan Peoples.
Page 95. Softplay
                                    by Alan Gillespie.
Page 97. The Canal
                                    by A J Kennedy.
Page 103. More beautiful by the hour
                         A sonnet by Barney MacFarlane.
Page 104. The Memory Man
                                    by Hugh V. McLachlan.
Page 112. You are Loved
                                    by Annie Healy.
Page 113. Hogmanay
                                    by Deborah Portilla.
Page 115. close
                                    by Sean McGarvey.
Page 117. More than a battlefield
                                    by Samantha Booth.
Page 122. The Waiting Rom
                                    by Jonathan Aitken.
Page 123. Stuck In the Middle
                                    by Bill Brown.
Page 128. Poppies
                                    by Erin Jamieson.
Page 129. One Bite of Me
                                    by Jane Jay Morrison.

PREFACE

Battlefield Writers was created by Alex Meikle and Frank Chambers in the Battlefield area of Glasgow's southside. The aim was to bring together local writers and produce a collection of short stories and poems. That first book, Tales from the Battlefield, had eleven different contributors.

This collection has twenty-nine different contributors and as we go to print the collective has grown to over thirty writers, both local and from beyond the Battlefield.
The editorial team were Alex Meikle, Frank Chambers and Palma McKeown. Cover design by Annie Bidault.

Find out more at

www.battlefieldwriters.com

A Growing Doubt

By Maureen Myant

Emma lay awake in the dark, unable to sleep. When she closed her eyes, worries flooded in: debris from the wreck of her life. When she opened them, it was to stare into the gloom of their hotel room in Samarkand. Tom's shorts were hanging up by the open window. They flapped crow-like in the draught from the balcony. A light from outside was reflected in the mirror. For a momentary miss of a heartbeat, she was sure there was a face, watching her, but she blinked, and it disappeared.

Tom was fast asleep, snoring. Emma screwed her elbow into the small of his back; he grunted and turned over, his breathing settling into a quieter, steadier rhythm. Emma stretched her legs across the bed searching for a cool spot on the sheets, but there was none. With careful, fluid movements so as not to wake Tom, she slid out of bed and trudged to the bathroom, closing the door before she put on the light. The glare blinded her for several seconds before she could see properly. Her face in the mirror was the colour of putty. Emma turned on the cold tap and held her hands under it as a scoop. She splashed tepid water over her face and scrutinised the shadows under her eyes. They were dark and translucent at the same time, ink smudged by a tear. She soaked her facecloth and wrung it out.

Back in bed, the sheets were warm and crumpled. Emma smoothed the bottom one, placed the facecloth on her forehead and lay down.

The dial of the hotel clock glowed with an eerie luminescence. Two thirty. Twenty minutes since she had returned to bed. Her facecloth was already dry, rough, and fibrous against her skin. She flicked it away and turned her pillow over. Thought stoppers, that's what was needed…

sandbags to keep her worries away: counting backwards in threes, reversing the alphabet, trying to recall the registration numbers of every car she'd ever owned. She'd tried them all, but nothing worked. Her anxieties seeped back like water from a blocked drain. Resigned, Emma reached for her dressing gown; another night in the bathroom, diverting herself with a book.

At six o'clock when others were waking, she stumbled back to bed where she fell instantly into a light, troubled sleep.

'Time for a quickie before we get up?' Tom's voice was near her ear. She shivered despite the early morning heat.

She glanced at the clock, moved away from him, 'Later, Tom. There's not enough time now.'

He grabbed her round the waist and pulled her towards him. 'Come on, it's been a week.'

'Five days,' she corrected him.

'Aha, so you've been counting too.' His hand travelled down her body; she pushed it away. He kissed the nape of her neck, watching for a reaction. 'You know you want to. It'll only take a minute.'

'Now there's an offer I can refuse.' She smiled, willing him to back down.

He sighed, 'OK, you win. But later…'

Emma jumped out of bed, using the little energy she had. 'Great. Now, get up and get dressed.'

They travelled by bus to Registan Square. The air conditioning wasn't working and within minutes most of their group were using maps, books, anything, as fans. Their frantic flapping did nothing to disperse the clogging air. If anything, the heat increased. Emma leaned her forehead against the cool glass of the windowpane and studied the scenery. A row of poplars stood like sentinels along the side of the road. She looked for movement, a promise of a breeze, but they were as still as a photograph.

When they alighted from the bus the sun beat down on them. Emma's scalp prickled as if someone was stabbing a thousand pins into her skull. Stupefied by fatigue, she'd forgotten her hat. Tom handed her a linen handkerchief, folded into a triangle, and she placed it over her hair, tying it at the back of her neck. That was better; she put on her sunglasses and scanned the square.

It was vast, a dazzling, magnificent scene. One side of the square, where they were standing, was open. The other three sides were outlined by Madrassas, Islamic teaching colleges. Their minarets were studded with mosaics and the cerulean domes blurred into the cloudless sky. On the ground in front of the buildings, mulberry trees provided much needed shade.

Tom brushed his hair back from his forehead. 'Doesn't this make you feel humble?'

'What do you mean?'

'All this was built hundreds of years ago. Look at the skill involved. Here we are in the twenty-first century, and I can't even put up a garden shed without it falling down.'

He wasn't exaggerating. Emma smiled. 'We all have different skills,' she said, 'yours is accountancy.'

'That's right. Remind me what a boring old fart I am. I add up figures, others put together fantastic buildings like this.' He waved a hand at the square. 'Do you think the people who worked on this thought it would be here centuries later?'

Emma's head throbbed in the heat. She rummaged through her handbag. Hadn't she put some paracetamol in there this morning? 'I don't know. Surely they did it for the glory of God? They wouldn't think about their own part in it.' She found the packet, popped two out from their sealed bubbles into her mouth.

Tom sighed. 'It must be wonderful to leave something like this. A sign that you've been here.'

Oh God, not this again. Time to change the subject. 'Give me your phone and I'll take a picture of you.'

Tom gripped her arm, 'Do you ever regret marrying me?'

She looked down at her shoes. They were covered in dust. Ashes to ashes, she thought, till death do us part. 'Of course not,' she said, 'Why would I?'

'You know why.' His grip tightened.

'I've told you before; I don't have a maternal gene.' Her voice was light.

'You say that, but you don't mean it.'

Sunglasses masked his eyes; his expression hidden but she didn't need to see it to know it would be sad. He had been devastated when he came down with mumps, a year after their marriage. 'I do mean it.' And she did. She'd been ambivalent about children. Not like Tom.

'Are you sure?'

'Yes.' Emma kissed him on the cheek. He had to believe her.

They walked on in silence, a little behind the rest of the group, and caught up with them at the Sher-Dor Madrassa. Tom went inside, leaving Emma standing in front of the portal. She gazed up at the arch, taking in its intricate mosaics of leonine animals and tried to concentrate on her guidebook.

It was too hot, so she joined Tom inside the ancient building where it was cool and tranquil. She could sleep here. Tom was in the middle, looking up at the ceiling. Emma paused behind him and whispered, 'Please be happy with what we have.' He took her hand and squeezed it, much too hard.

Back at the hotel, there was time for a rest before dinner. Emma fell asleep as soon as she lay down on the bed. When she awoke, Tom was sitting on the only chair, her phone in his hand. She squinted at him.

'What are you doing?'

'I could ask you the same thing.' His voice was hard, unforgiving.

Emma sunk into the mattress, too tired to argue, but Tom wasn't prepared to give up that easily. He looked down at the phone and read, 'We need to talk. You shouldn't be going on holiday.' Damn, she should have deleted the text. What had she been thinking? Emma knew the words by heart; she'd gone over them in her head for almost a week, wondering if she'd done the right thing.

'You've been going through my handbag.'

He ignored the outrage in her voice, tried to keep the moral high ground. 'Who's it from?'

It wasn't the right time for this discussion. She'd wanted to get their holiday over first. 'Not that it's any of your business,' she muttered, 'but it's from a colleague. We've been very short staffed.' She worked in a hospital. It wasn't a total lie.

He stared at her. He wanted to believe her, and she seized the advantage. Her own gaze was unblinking as she willed him to accept her word. Tom shook his head. 'Were they trying to get you to work through your holidays?'

She had to make him believe this. 'Yes.'

Tom crossed the room, crouched by the bed. 'I'm sorry, but you've been so distant recently… I started to think there was someone else. I couldn't bear it you know… if you left me.'

She wanted to say *I'll always be there for you,* but the words remained unspoken.

They went down to dinner in silence. Emma was resigned to sex later. It was impossible to put it off any longer. As he kept reminding her, it had been nearly a week. They'd never gone that long without making love. All her excuses were as tired as she was: too early, too late, too hot, headaches, tummy upsets. She picked at her food, barely listening to the conversation around her. When she pushed the plate away, she caught Tom staring at her, and her stomach tightened. He had a way of looking at her from underneath lowered eyebrows: intimate and knowing. Whenever he did that, no matter where they were, it's as if he was undressing her. Across the table he mouthed *I want you* and she blushed, longing for him, in spite of everything.

Back in their room, Tom drew her into his arms, kissed her, tracing her face with his finger. Emma presses her body against his. She could do this. She could manage without him finding out. She fell back onto the bed with him on top. He started to undress her, but she pushed his hands away. 'I'll do it,' she said, twisting round to switch off the light.

He stopped her. 'Why so shy? There's nothing I haven't seen before.'

An uneasy smile, 'No, of course not.'

Tom frowned. 'You're hiding something. What is it? A love bite?'

If only it were that simple. Emma switched off the light once more, forced a laugh and pulled him down on top of her. His hands stroked her breasts, she stiffened, but he didn't notice.

Afterwards, Emma waited for his questions. He must have felt it; he held her breast in his hand, fondled and squeezed it. She tried to think what to say, but there was no reasonable excuse for not having told him. Unable to bear the silence any longer she whispered, 'Tom?' No reply. She raised herself up on one elbow, peered down at him. He was asleep.

Emma lay down. For a moment she let herself believe everything was fine; he didn't feel it, so it wasn't there. She raised her right hand and looked at it. Long, elegant fingers, manicured nails, taut, smooth skin; the hand of a young woman. She allowed it to stray towards her left breast. Fanning her fingers out, she traced round her nipple, feeling the puckering of the skin. The lump was still there, a hard, grainy nodule near the surface. She pressed down hard, but it didn't go.

TINY PIN CUSHION WUMIN

by Greg Shearer

O' tiny pin cushion wumin,
Patron saint ae NHS surgeries,
A hod yer hawn as we cross the street.
Time's hawns caress ye
Wae fingertips ae broken gless,
Leave ye like colouring book pages
In hospital waitin' rooms.
Ye laugh sometimes sayin'
Ye ought tae be Shelley's Eve,
Bruised like a peach, cut like a lemon,
Held the gither wae costume jewellery,
Tea wae two Sweetex
And lust fur life.
Ye've never been anyhin but beautiful
A've never known any different or better,
Since long a'fore the creep of age,
A'fore the sickly stream of result letters,
A'fore the cancer and the transplants,
A'fore the surgeries and the suffrage,
A'fore the sainthood,
And survival, still efter,
Ye would never be any less than whole,
Holy, wholly mine,
Ma mum.
O' tiny pin cushion wumin,
A miss like ma ain milk teeth the days,
When you held ma hawn as we crossed the street.

WRITER'S RETREAT
By Carolyn Mandache

What do you get when you cross one boring academic breaking into fiction, one weirdo sci-fi wannabe, one token murder mystery writer, one annoyingly bubbly rom-com writer and one shit-don't-stink children's author? The makings of a writer's retreat to remember, or more accurately... one impossible to forget.

"Daisy, leave poor Amanda alone you big goofball!"

"Oh, don't worry, I love dogs." I lied. The beast looked like it should be in a fucking stable. Daisy licked my hand. I thought dogs were supposed to make good judges of character.

The lodge was homely and comforting, made the short ferry ride worthwhile. She clapped her hands loudly.

"Welcome, welcome to all of you and I hope you're all as excited as I am for the creative weekend ahead."

"Just a quick run through of the itinerary for the weekend, and then you're free to go and settle into your rooms. We'll meet back here in an hour for our first writing exercise. Does that sound ok?"

I nodded my agreement along with my fellow writers.

"Super! So, I'll keep today's exercise top secret for now, and then it's afternoon tea outside with that spectacular view." Her arm dramatically gestured to the window behind her and the morons around me took the bait; "It really is stunning…"

"Yes, you can see why Scotland's one of the most beautiful places in the world."

Tamara smiled smugly, as if she'd personally been sub-contracted by God to create Arran herself.

. . . .

"How's your room Amanda?" I felt her eyes bore into me, then remembered that I was Amanda, at least for now.

"Oh…sorry! Away in a world of my own there." She beamed at me, pleased to have found another dizzy daydreamer no doubt. Pretty sure my daydreams would eat hers alive.

"Daisy not up for any writing just now?"

She laughed more than my quip had earned, I forced my eyes not to roll in my head.

"No, no, think she's tired out from the journey, I'll take her a long walk later."

"Good idea, maybe I'll join you? What was your name again?"

"Jessica."

The chit chat around about us died down as Tamara gave her signature clap again.

So far, I'd endured three horrendous book ideas. Katie's "hilarious" rom-com idea, Edward's ridiculous sci-fi synopsis, and Jessica's latest addition to her Poppy Petal picture books.

"Amanda, how about your future bestselling idea?" The group turned to face me, smiling that familiar way that any regular attendee at a retreat recognises; encouraging, with a hint of fear that the story will make their idea pale into insignificance.

"Oh, it's silly really." Nothing like a bit of self-doubt to make competitors view you as a nothing...non-threatening...harmless.

"No silly ideas here Amanda." I spouted off one of my many horrendous plot variations concocted over the years.

"Well...that's certainly different Amanda. Can't wait to hear more about it! OK as you'll know, the group takes turns preparing the meals, so.... let me just check my list."

"Katie and Edward, your turn tonight. Now, an important reminder; someone in the group has a serious allergy, so please be very mindful of the ingredients you use." She peered over her glasses at the 2 cooks to make sure they acknowledged the information she'd just relayed.

Jessica paused at the doorway and looked back over her shoulder towards me. "You fancy joining me for that walk now?"

"Sure, let me just grab my coat."

Daisy almost knocked me off my feet when she saw me. I longed to pull tight on her red lead, not only stop the barking, but her breathing too.

"So...Poppy Petal? Sounds like kids love those stories."

"Well yeah, they do but..." I watched closely as Jessica bit her lip, and wondered what this little miss goody two shoes could possibly be worried about saying.

"But what?" I pretended to be watching Daisy, took the focus away from Jessica to make her believe it was her choice to speak or not.

"I have an idea for a novel, something really dark that no one would believe I could write! I'm not even sure I can do it myself, but the idea just won't go away. Coming here, I thought I'd have the courage to talk about it, make a start you know?"

I nodded encouragingly as she looked up at me with Bambi eyes.

"But how can the writer of Poppy Petal, move onto something so completely out of my comfort zone?"

"I get that. Tell your idea and they might be supportive, or they might tear it to shreds." A look of defeat crossed her face providing me with a warm pleasant glow.

"Look. How about you use me as a sounding board? You can trust me. I won't say anything to anyone."

"Promise you won't laugh?"

A hint of a smile, I'd won her round.

"Ok; here goes."

Jessica took a deep breath and launched into the most twisted, original and intriguing storyline I had ever heard. I listened intently to her passionately explain the plot, which most definitely was "off-brand". Amazing what people are capable of if you scratch beneath the surface, the hidden depths to their personalities.

"Jessica, have you told anyone this idea? Anyone at all?"

"No, I told you, I've been too scared. You're the only one who knows. I haven't even written anything down, it's all up here." Jessica tapped the side of her head.

This is it Rebecca, you've finally found your muse.

"Jessica, that book must be written. It's…well, it's bloody brilliant!"

Her cheeks, already flushed with the cold, reddened a deeper shade as a broad smile lit up her pretty, sickeningly innocent face.

"Just a few words of advice; don't share your idea with anyone from the group. Trust me, someone would steal that exceptional plotline, without a second thought."

"Not me, of course Jessica. You can trust me 100%" a quick hand on the heart for extra effect.

Daisy seemed to have worked off her boundless energy and we walked back to the lodge as the last of the daylight faded.

"I'm just gonna make a coffee to heat up a bit, Jessica. See you at dinner."

I headed to the small kitchen, turning on the tap to fill the kettle. I'd kept a close eye on Tamara earlier, conveniently she'd left the cooking rota on the magnetic noticeboard. Pulling it down, I flicked the page over for the information I needed. My finger followed the line along to see which unfortunate had such a modern-day health issue. Slowly I closed my eyes, a satisfied smile working its way across my face.

. . . .

"Amanda and Jessica, I have you two down for tonight's cooking. That works for you both?"

"Yes, fine, not a problem Tamara."

Katie and Edward's efforts the previous night had been surprisingly edible, then again, Tamara hadn't taken any chances. The lodge was stocked with designer meal kits, perfectly proportioned ingredients, and fool proof instructions.

Peeking into our box of goodies I was pleased to see we were lucky enough to have an Italian theme for our turn. Little boxes of herbs and spices, fresh pasta, passata and organic veggies, there was even fresh dough to make our own garlic bread. Everything was securely sealed, but Jessica wouldn't know that. Pulling the unsalted peanuts from my bag, I battered it over and over against the edge of the table. I whizzed the peanut fragments into a fine powder using the food processor. Adding a little to each container and mixing well, I was confident there was no visible trace or smell of the allergen. Closing all the containers to look good as new I took a quick look at the instruction sheet. Just as I'd hoped, the bold warning was there for all to see: "may contain traces of nuts". I headed upstairs for a soothing cup of tea, the calm before the storm.

. . . .

"Cheers Jessica." The glasses clinked together, a toast to a potentially lucrative, if short-lived friendship.

"I'll make the dough for the garlic bread if you want to start the pasta sauce."

The setup couldn't be better. Poor sods with allergies can come out in hives even touching the offending food, so this designer cooking malarky was perfect. Everything was measured out, no need to touch a damn thing, except the dough of course.

Onions and garlic sizzled in olive oil, juicy red tomatoes and crisp pepper slices. The smell was divine, and my stomach growled with eager anticipation for the meal to come. In went the ore-gano, ore-gano as she pronounced it and of course, plenty of my secret ingredient.

"You want to taste it so far?" Jessica held out a wooden spoon invitation.

"Pretty good I'd say, yeah." I dropped the spoon back into the saucepan, knowing full well Jessica would want the utensil washed first. The scolding was too cute.

Seated at the table I took a deep, calming breath. I wanted to be in the perfect frame of mind to enjoy the show.

Impossible to know how bad her reaction would be, but Tamara had warned of a serious allergy.

No one seemed to notice how quiet I was. Her cheeks were flushed; from the wine or the first indication of her body realising something wasn't quite right? I started an internal count, how long until the nuts took effect? I'd always liked chemistry, watching my live experiment was thrilling.

She cleared her throat and my heart leapt... false alarm. Taking a forkful of pasta, I chewed slowly to appreciate the flavours, my eyes locked on Jessica sat opposite me. I had the best seat in the house.

Another forkful to her mouth, and another; 10, 11, 12…a gulp of wine; 13, 14, 15, drunken giggling at Michael's pathetic joke; 16, 17, 18, 19, 20. Then it happened, 21… such a special number. I hadn't expected it to be so deliciously theatrical, but my God… it was hypnotic!

The frightened eyes, wider than seemed humanly possible, the desperate, rasping breaths more difficult with each inhale, the slender, manicured hands clawing at her uncooperative throat as it closed over…drowning, whilst nowhere near water. The instant panic as our dinner guests tried to work out the problem. Tamara's hands shaking uncontrollably by her sides "It can't be her allergy. I took every precaution with those kits."

"Well, clearly it is Tamara! Where's her damn epi-pen?" Michael had instantly sobered up, his sharp voice shocked Tamara into action, knocking her chair over as she left to find Jessica's handbag.

I knew exactly where it was, wedged between the sofa cushions where I'd put it. There was a tiny bit of strap still showing as a little clue; I'm not a complete monster. I put my calming arm around Jessica.

"Everything's going to be fine, you'll see." I caught my smile just in time.

"I've got it! I've got it!" Tamara held up the lilac fluffy handbag. Watching her rifle through its contents was delightful.

"It's…it's not here!" Her head jerked up, alert and horrified at the same time.

"Give me that!" Michael took control and grabbed the bag from Tamara's shaking hands. The remainder of the contents tumbled out as he tipped the bag upside down, desperately shaking it even after it was clear there was nothing left inside.

Katie heaved the heavy velvet seat pads off the sofa. "It must have fallen down the couch somewhere."

"Find her room key, she must have somehow left it upstairs." Katie had abandoned the couch search and was now on a new mission in Operation Save Jessica.

"Tamara, stay here with Jessica, I'll go help look for the pen." A reassuring squeeze to her shoulder and I was off.

Footsteps thundered up the stairs as we headed for her room.

The final act was better than I could ever have hoped. As I said, it's astonishing how much info people will give away once you have their trust. That's how I'd discovered exactly what she needed to do if her allergy flared up. The epi-pen was always with her, and a spare stored in the top drawer of her room. She'd even pulled it out to show me on the walk earlier, the bright orange cap making it easy to find in emergencies... or so she thought. All I'd had to do was bring her a cup of coffee and make my move when she went to the toilet. The stupid dog had watched me, head cocked to one side wondering what I was up to. I'd found the spare and the one in her handbag, then made my excuses to leave.

"What's wrong with Daisy?" Katie bent down beside the beast, gently ruffling her head. The ears moved of their own accord, but nothing else. She gasped and quickly withdrew her hand.

"Never mind the bloody dog, we need to find that pen!" Michael started rummaging through drawers, Jessica's clothes, down the back of the bed; anywhere he could think of. The rest of us remained frozen to the spot.

"There's...there's something under Daisy's paw." Edward pointed to the floor where something peeked out from under the giant limb...something orange. Seemed only fitting that I should be the one to reveal the punchline to my twisted story. Completely mangled but still recognisable I held it up with my best horrified expression, a few last drops of the magic liquid which could have saved Jessica ran down my fingers.

"Wait a minute! I've just remembered her saying she had a spare somewhere." The false hope kicked them back into gear, frantically searching every nook and cranny.

"I found it." Edward's voice was subdued and distant. Not the voice of someone about to save a life, if there even was a life still to be saved. Slowly he held up a second barely recognisable pen, the orange lid, the only clear identifying feature.

"Where was it?"

"Under Daisy's head." He looked apologetically to the dead animal, like he pitied it.

I'd returned the pens to Jessica's room before we started cooking. The big brute had been delighted at my special treats; two epi-pens delightfully smothered in jelly from his favourite dog food. This was my second experiment, and I was delighted with the result. I hadn't worried there'd be any evidence of my tampering, knew that dumb dog would lick those things sparkling clean, and of course I'd hoped she'd decide they made a good chew toy...tick, tick. Would two epi-pens contain enough medicinal liquid to kill a dog of this size? Clearly, the answer was yes.

The ambulance siren brought us all back to our senses as they headed back downstairs in dread, myself on a giddy high.

Tamara stretched her arms out in desperation beside a silent, passed out Jessica "Quick! Where's the pen?"

The ding dong of the doorbell interrupted the bearing of bad news, as the paramedics took control.

"She's had a reaction to the meal, and we...couldn't find the epi-pens." Michael briefed the experts, leaving out the grim Daisy details for the time being, to spare Tamara any more upset.

"The dog chewed them to bits." I tried to sound distressed, but admittedly it could have come out as excitement. I watched Tamara's eyes grow almost as wide as Jessica's had mid-reaction.

"There's a faint pulse. What kind of pen was it?" The paramedic looked around for answers.

Edward held out the corpse of the pen he'd found, the paramedic's eyebrows rose in surprise.

"There were more? Any others in a better state? Pretty hard to make out anything identifiable on that thing and I need to make sure she gets the right one." His partner, a woman who looked too young to hold such a responsible job was frantically googling epi-pens.

"Helen, put that phone away, there's no pulse, we need to start CPR."

Quickly she shoved the phone in her pocket and began chest compressions, as her partner kept count. The room fell silent as everyone, minus one, prayed for a heartbeat.

Gently the older paramedic put his hand on Helen's arm, "Ok, that's enough Helen." Looking at his watch, I knew what his next words would be.

"Time of death, 7.13p.m."

The police arrived soon afterwards, took statements from everyone.

The retreat was over, everyone wanted away from the unimaginable tragedy, and we each went our separate ways. I was confident that any creative juices were now well and truly dried up…at least for them. Personally, I couldn't wait to put pen to paper.

Prospecthill Road
by Kathryn Metcalfe

Take my word for it

there are goldfinches,

baubles of yellow and red

feather festooning bare

branches of a rowan tree,

lighting up

a brittle December day.

The Sane Scientist's New Invention
By Jane Jay Morrison

The scientist – who definitely wasn't mad - unveiled his incredible new invention: a vehicle powered entirely by the vibrational energy of purring cats!

"This renewable and theoretically limitless source of energy will change the world," cried the scientist, completely sanely, to the awe-struck journalists and photographers crowding around. "Twenty years hence, *all* vehicles will be cat-purr-powered!"

Paparazzi snapped, crowds cheered, children pointed, and news-reporters gabbled. The maiden voyage began! Behind the driver's cab, where the scientist steered, zoomed a vast lorry-sized platform. Within, a hundred cardboard-lined, cashmere-layered, catnip-perfumed luxury pigeonholes. In each, a gloved, mechanical, feline-petting arm. Each pivot of its steel-screwed elbow was programmed to scritch the head of its delighted white or brindled or calico or ginger resident at perfectly calculated trigonometric angles, extracting maximum purr. The whole *road* vibrated as they flew along!

"More! Faster!" cackled the scientist (because that was clearly a perfectly mentally healthy thing to do). "We're running at no less than three hundred ticklewatts of purr energy!"

And then, *disaster*. The horrified scientist realized, too late, the major design flaw. He should *not* have assumed his fuzzy energy-sources would be too content to move. They should *not* have had access to the driver's cab. The engine stalled.

"O, *fuck*," said the scientist. It was the sanest thing he'd said yet.

Screaming and thrashing, he disappeared under a tidal wave of toe-beans, as *one hundred* loved-up cats all tried to sit on his lap at once! The vehicle lurched and skidded awhile. The appalled audience gasped. "News just in," cried the TV reporters. "There's nothing left of him!"

When the wreckage was investigated, and the hundred still-purring cats removed to a shelter, all that remained of the flattened scientist was his white lab-coat, slightly bloodstained.

And horribly in need of a lint-brush.

All Inclusive

By Colette Coen

'You told them, didn't you? That it was the guy from Glasgow that sent you?'

They look a bit sheepish, but Patricia says, 'It was lovely. You were right. We would never have found it in the old town ourselves.'

I know John looks scary with his protein-pumped body and his shaved head, so it's nice if I add a little comfort. 'Glasgow's got the best curries in Europe,' I say. 'Maybe even the world,' (though we've never been to India) 'Bradford, Birmingham, Glasgow – we all know how to make curries.'

'Chicken Tikka Masala was invented in Glasgow. Did you know that?' John says with a wee nudge to Steve. The couple nod, smile, and I can see they're not quite sure what to do next, maybe they're wondering if they can boast about Wigan, but it's okay, John's moved on.

'I'll get you a drink,' John says, acting as mein host, even though we're all-inclusive.

'Sangria,' Patricia says.

But John won't hear of it, 'Has to be a Mojito here, Patsy,' he says, 'best on the Algarve.'

I smile at Patricia and give her a look of assurance while John places the order. Mojitos for the girls, beer and a chaser for the boys. We've not seen this barman before, so John introduces himself, leaning over the bar to shake Joseph's hand. 'John, Brenda, from Glasgow.'

Steve sips his beer, and I can see his sideways glance to Patricia, like they're using telepathy to figure out how best to get away from us.

'This is the first time we've been away without the kids,' Patricia says, and I can see that this will later be woven into an excuse about them wanting to spend some time together alone. 'Thought the day would never come,' she says with a nervous laugh.

'How many children do you have?' I ask, as is expected of me.

'Twin boys,' she says, and again, that laugh.

'That was enough,' Steve says, 'got the snip once I realised, she was having them two at a time.'

'They've gone off with friends this year,' Patricia says, ignoring her husband, 'but I'm making sure they stay in touch.'

'Where they off to?' John asks, gulping down more beer. 'Ibiza, is it? We had some great times there when we were younger – a couple of Es and then raving all night. Prefer the beer myself now. Couldn't drink with those drugs. Had to be water or you would kill yourself, and that's no way to end a holiday.'

'Zante,' Patricia says, and John looks at her like he's forgotten the question he asked.

I know where his thoughts are, because mine are there too. Ibiza, that first year, when our high school flirting got serious, led to us swapping rooms with our pals, which worked out well – okay, maybe not for them. I came home without a tan that year. Had to tell my folks that it was too hot to sunbathe.

'Probably clubbing all night and sleeping all day,' my dad decided, and I left it at that.

We went to San Antonio again on our honeymoon, and for a couple of years after that, until we reckoned that the clubbers were getting younger, and the music was nowhere near as good.

'What line of business are you in yourself Steve?' John asks, although we had this conversation a couple of nights ago when John gave them his recommendations for the Indian restaurant, and a couple of Irish bars in the town. 'We've been here a few times you see.'

'I run a small software firm,' Steve says, and John makes a joke about Bill Gates, the same one he made the first time Steve told him, though a Steve's job joke would have been better.

'Oh, Brenda's into all that high-tech stuff,' John says, 'never quite mastered it myself.' He wears it as a badge of honour, like he's getting on fine without knowing how to operate in the world.

'Don't know how we survived before,' Patricia says. 'I wouldn't be able to sleep at night if I couldn't skype the boys. I love the Kindle for my books too – so much lighter when you're reading by the pool. Can't get them wet though, must read my mags in the bath these days rather than my Fifty Shades."

'Need to let them stretch their wings though, don't you?' John says, 'Cut the apron strings.'

I had my first miscarriage in Benidorm. I'd been off the pill for a couple of years and was so excited when I finally saw the blue line that we nearly cancelled the holiday. I read in the books that a bit of bleeding in the first few weeks wasn't anything to worry about, spotting, they called it, but it worried me enough to talk to the rep. A young girl, she was, who looked panicked and said she'd need to check with her supervisor. Next thing the supervisor was knocking on our hotel door and taking me to the local clinic to act as a translator.

The second one was three years later in Salou. John said I shouldn't go on anything too scary at Port Aventura, but I'd been bleeding for two days by then and needed an excuse why I'd failed again.

I compliment Patricia's dress and she thanks me without telling me where she got it, or how much it cost. 'Yours is lovely too,' she says, although a returned compliment doesn't mean that much.

'I'm in Sales,' John says, 'cars mainly.' It's been a while since anyone gave him a chance, but it gives him an in with

Steve, so I let it go. 'What do you drive yourself? You look like an Audi man. Am I right?'

'Used to be,' Steve says, 'more Uber these days.'

'Lost your licence, did you? Too much of the old beer.'

'Epilepsy,' Patricia says, with a clip to it. 'I've got a Golf.' She recovers. 'Runs like a dream.'

'You all right, Sean?' John shouts over to a man who has just come into the bar with his wife. Sean waves, and they go to sit in the corner, using the self-serve machines for drinks on their way.

'Top notch guy, that Sean. Watched the football with him the other night. A Scouser, you know, never met one of them yet who wasn't decent.'

'We're off home tomorrow,' I say, just to reassure Patricia and Steve that they won't have to endure us much longer.

We like holidays, take them whenever we can, although since John stopped working, we've not been able to go as far, or for as long. He likes to plan them, jokes that he should become a travel agent, though we both know that's becoming less likely with every passing month. He scores through the dates in his diary when we book the tickets, implying that there might be other pressures on his time. He still likes me to do the shopping for new clothes, can't really cope with busy places where he might bump into someone he used to know.

And I love hotels. The change in scenery always does us the power of good, just like the experts tell you. I like the fact that I don't have to cook, not like at home, when I come in exhausted from work and John hasn't been about to rouse himself. I like that the toilets are cleaned, and sins washed down the drain; carpets are hoovered and the bills can wait. Most of all I like the two single beds tucked in so tight that it would seem rude to disturb them. It's too hot for sex anyway, even with the air conditioning, or John's too drunk, or I'm too burnt.

His bonhomie had disappeared by the time we got to the airport. It has been dripping out of him with sweat since early morning, although he did manage a couple, "You okay big man." as we made our way down the TUI coach. 'Stomach's a bit dodgy myself,' he said to give everyone a reason why his new friends don't immediately come to share his company.

By the time the flight has been called he can barely stand. It gets him that way sometimes, and he slumps into his seat on the plane, and only orders tea when the stewardess comes round. I can already tell this is going to be a bad one.

He can't understand how I can enjoy teaching – watching other people's children learn and grow gives me pleasure, when it would only give him pain. He doesn't understand how I can enjoy anything when life is so hopeless and people only ever see the worst of each other, and the world is so full of evil, that he can't believe that people can get out of bed in the morning.

And besides, I like the school holidays. Means I can spend time with John, keep an eye on him. Make sure he doesn't do anything stupid.

I hold his hand as we come down to land. 'It's going to be okay, love. I've got you.

Padraig – Who Drove the Snakes Out of Ireland
by Pratibha Castle

At the allotment, daddy

forked the crumbly black earth

till the air quaked

with anticipation

of excess, me

sifting stones

in search of treasure;

the robin sat, pert, on the lip

of the bucket meant

to carry spuds or cabbages,

the occasional giggle-tickle carrot

back to placate the mammy.

The bird's eye bright

with a lust for worms, his song

a crystal cataract of merry; though

none of the seeds we sowed ever

showed head out of the sly earth

and we saw nothing

of the slow worm

daddy promised so that,

his name being Padraig too,

I guessed he must be a saint,

especially when he himself vanished.

Though he turned up months later

at the end of school

again and again and again

till I had to tell the mammy

where the books and toys came from

and that got me sent off

to board at St. Bridget's convent

where the head nun was nice to you

if your mammy gave her fruit cake in a tin,

bottles of orange linctus sherry,

a crocheted shawl

like frothy cobwebs,

none of which my mammy could afford,

Padraig having banished more than snakes.

First published in A Triptych of Birds & A Few Loose Feathers (Hedgehog Poetry Press)

Rags to Rags in Three Generations
By Frank Chambers

'"Ice cream or chips?" That's what he asked me. "Ice cream or chips?"'

Carla is outraged at this clear example of racial stereotyping and makes to say so. The old man shakes his head and raises his hand to stop her.

'It was a long time ago. A long, long time ago. That's just how it was back then, no point in going on about it. We Italians had worse than that to put up with, I can tell you. Much worse. There are things even your grandfather was never told about. We never spoke of such things.

Anyway, it was my first day at the secondary school, August nineteen forty. Me and a hundred other boys standing in the playground, scared out of our wits, waiting to be allocated our classes. Mr Mulrooney, the Deputy Head, was standing at the top of the steps, dressed in his black gown, and clutching a bunch of papers, all flapping about in the wind. He shouts, "Silence," then begins to bark out names as if he was a sergeant major addressing a bunch of new recruits. When he gets to my name, he pauses, noticing that it is Italian, then he pronounces it badly. Mulrooney waits until I step forward, before demanding to know. "Ice cream or chips?"'

Again, Carla makes to speak, and again Peppino's hand is raised. She smiles and gives in graciously. The family business was in trouble and Carla had come to the patriarch of the family for advice and guidance, not to fight old battles. Giuseppe, but always known as Peppino, was her grandfather's older cousin and just three days short of his ninety fifth birthday. His experience and wisdom would be brought to bear on the problem, Carla was certain of that, but it would be in his own good time, it always was. Carla resigned herself to the wait and sank back into the Parker Knoll chair, placed beside the bed and made herself comfortable.

"'Ice cream or chips?' I could hardly get angry with the man. How could I? It was perfectly true after all. I didn't even need to answer his question. Before I had the chance to open my mouth, half the boys shouted out, "chips". That was my nickname from that day forward.

I'm only telling you this Carla, because I asked your grandfather that very same question, a quarter of a century later. It was the night Tony arrived from Italy. I had picked him up at Glasgow Central Station and we were in the car, making our way back to Hamilton. The date was, November second, nineteen sixty-seven. Do you know that date?'

Carla shook her head.

'Well, you should. It is the most important date for your family's business, and perhaps for Scotland too.' Peppino pushed himself up in the bed so that his head was now above Carla's, who had sunk further into the chair as she awaited one of Peppino's 'stories.'

"'Ice cream or chips?" I said. "That's where the money is, at least for us Italians. That is where the family can help you Tony. No one knows fish and chips better than us. As for ice cream, well who better than Cousin Massimo. Nothing would make him happier than to help someone in the family starting out in business." Your grandfather just shrugged his shoulders and said, "I don't know Peppino, I've got some ideas of my own. Something I saw in the movies."

Before I had a chance to ask him what on earth he was talking about, Tony had spotted the large crowds gathered outside the Town Hall. "What's going on there?" he asked.

"Oh, they're waiting for the result of the by-election," I said. "The SNP are standing."

"What's the SNP?" Tony asked.

29

I had to explain to him who the SNP were, and that they had decided to put up a candidate against Labour and the Conservatives this time, even though they hadn't even stood at the general election the year before.

"Let's stop and see if they win," Tony says.

"The count could take hours," I protested.'

Carla had never known her grandfather to take even the tiniest bit of interest in politics, but she didn't interrupt, there would be some point to Peppino's tale. All would be revealed, eventually.

'Your grandfather was so excited. The TV cameras were there you see, and the newspaper reporters and photographers.

"They're not going to win," I told him. "Hamilton has been Labour since the war."

"But they might," Tony says. "At least they're trying something different, not just giving the people the same old choices."

"Same old choices?" Then I understood the point your grandfather was making. What he was really talking about was not Labour or Conservative. It was, "ice cream or chips."

Well! The SNP won and Winnie Ewing became an MP, the only Nationalist at Westminster. It was the biggest shock ever. Hamilton was world news.

The very next morning, over breakfast, Tony told me what his big idea was. He was going to sell pizza.

"Pizza!" I said. "People around here don't even know what a pizza looks like." I tried to put him off the idea, but he had seen it in a film set in New York and was convinced, if it worked there, it would work here.

"Scotland is not America." I told him, "And films are not real life." All the uncles and cousins said the same thing. Tony wouldn't listen.

"If they love pizza in New York, why won't they love pizza in Glasgow," Tony would say. There was no talking him out of it. His mind was made up.

Tony first tried to sell his pizzas in Uncle Luigi's chip shop in Bellshill. When that didn't work, he managed to persuade a cafe in Glasgow to let him sell his pizzas there, but it never really took off. He then took a job in a restaurant where he managed to talk the owner into putting pizza on the menu. That too ended in failure.

Tony got sacked from the restaurant job the very week that Winnie lost her seat at the general election. I said to Tony. "Scotland is not ready for the SNP, and it is not ready for pizza either." I told him, "Winnie should have joined the Labour Party, and you should have opened a chip shop. Life would have been a lot easier for the both of you." I said to your grandfather, "You could be living in a nice little house in Bothwell by now, with a garden and space to grow your own vegetables, not living in a draughty old tenement flat, among the students and long-haired hippies down in Glasgow."

Winnie and Tony, it seemed, were on parallel tracks. Like her, when Tony suffered a setback, he just picked himself up and tried again. They are the first generation, you see. The generation that gets something started. They see possibilities that no one else sees and they make things happen. Do you hear what I'm saying, Carla?'

Carla smiled. She could see where this was going. As far back as she could remember, there were stories about how papa Tony struggled in the early days. The first shop that was in the wrong place, the second shop that was too small. She had heard all about the ovens that weren't right for pizza, the problems getting the right kind of flour and all the different toppings her grandfather had used, trying to satisfy the Scottish palate. However, Peppino didn't say any of that.

'Tony could see inside people's heads, he understood what they really wanted, even when they didn't know it themselves. "If you make people feel good about themselves," he would say, "then you can sell them anything."

When Winnie got back into parliament in 1974, your grandfather saw it as a sign, and took out a lease on that first shop the very next week. The family all warned him against it, but Tony went ahead anyway. You know the story.' Carla nodded her head. 'But he never gave up. Tony was in that shop at seven in the morning and never left before midnight. Some nights there was barely a single customer. "Things will pick up," he would say, "it just takes a little time."

The first generation, remember! They keep on going till they get a break. For Winnie and the SNP, it was North Sea oil, for Tony it was the package holiday. Suddenly people had an appetite for foreign food, and they had discovered the delights of eating out in restaurants. It still took time to persuade them that pizza was a proper meal.

Things started to work for your grandfather when he opened the restaurant in the city centre. Tony ordered 300 giant plates from Italy for the sit in customers, and 18-inch cardboard boxes for take away. In that restaurant, that's where Tony perfected the formula. No one worked harder or did longer hours than Tony. He would turn his hands to any of the jobs, in the kitchen, behind the bar, or waiting the tables. If the cleaner didn't turn up, Tony would roll up his sleeves and get on with it himself. Step by step, he built up the business. Every regular customer, he knew by name, and would shout it out when they came through the door. He kept an old camera behind the counter. If anyone well known came in, he would get his picture taken beside them.'

Carla could remember seeing those old black and white pictures on the wall of the Glasgow restaurant, when she was a child. Faces off the television, pop stars and footballers, all pictured with her grandfather.

'Each year the takings were a little more than the one before. When that restaurant was running smooth as clockwork, he opened the place in the West End. That's about the time your father started working in the business, and soon after that, your aunt Carmela. Those were good times, happy times. Tony had a good steady business, nothing spectacular perhaps but, well, ……steady.

Now we get to the second generation.'

Carla could sense an implied criticism of her father in the tone of Peppino's voice and decided she had stayed silent long enough.

'It was during dad's time that the business expanded,' Carla exclaimed.

'And also, where it started to go wrong.'

'The business made more money after dad took over.'

'For a while, yes. I'm not criticising your father, Carla. Nor your aunt Carmela for that matter. When Tony retired, Gino and Carmela really stepped up to the mark. I'm not saying that they didn't. They had learned from the master, of course, and the hand over was as smooth as silk. Gino, I'll grant you, had some new tricks up his sleeve. He didn't wait for someone famous to walk through the door, he went out and found them. Gino would find out who was appearing at the theatres and concert halls each week and have a freshly baked pizza delivered to the stage door, with compliments of Tony's Pizzas. Nine times out of ten, he never heard a thing back, but every now and again, some actor or musician would turn up at the restaurant, just to say thank you or to buy another pizza. Gino always had a camera ready. He would send those pictures into the papers, who were more than willing to print them.

Gino became a celebrity and, I agree, business boomed. The restaurants were full of people, all hoping that some famous person would walk through the door. Sometimes, all they wanted was to get their own picture taken with Gino. But here's the thing, Carla. Image and celebrity were now the driving forces behind the business's success. Not pizza.

Your father and then Carmela did an exceptional job when they were in charge. I'm not disputing that. Gino and Carmela worked hard, opened new restaurants, made it work even at locations where nobody gave them a chance. Your father and your aunt, like Tony, knew their customers well. Like Tony they understood exactly what it was that made them tick.

They expanded the business, and they made some money. Enough for you, your brothers, and your cousins to have that private education. It worked well, but I still say that is where things started to go wrong. They were the second generation you see; it is easy for them. The second generation inherit a well-run business, all they must do is keep things going.'

Carla made to speak. Yet again, Peppino raised his hand.

'Please let me explain about the second generation. They inherit a good business, the fruits of someone else's labour and someone else's vision. Someone else's dream. If they are smart, they can tweak that winning formula, modernise perhaps, bring things up to date. If they are smart and lucky, the results appear spectacular. I have seen it many times when a family business passes down the generations. Things can go well for the second generation. They appear to have the Midas touch; they can do no wrong. Look at what happened with the SNP. But that is where the problems begin. If there is some difficulty, they may ask themselves what would the first generation have done? If the first generation had the right idea, the second generation can do what they think the first generation would have done. The trouble is, who do the third generation look to for guidance?'

Peppino had hit a nerve. Carla, even as a young teenager, could remember when visiting the restaurant, workers saying to dad, things like, "Tony wouldn't have done that," or "Tony did it like this." It was something of a bone of contention with her father, but on most occasions, he would go with the flow.

Carla expected Peppino to continue talking and the sudden silence took her unawares. 'Will I tell you the situation?'

'That's why you are here, is it not?'

'Well, yes.'

The speech Carla had written down, memorised and practised, was now lost in some corner of her brain. Jumbled snippets sloshed about her head, but not the first sentence, not even the first word. The more Carla tried to remember, the further away the information seemed to recede. Peppino was waiting. She would have to say something.

'It's my cousin! He's totally useless.' The words were blurted out, it was not at all what she had intended to say. Carla closed her eyes in embarrassment and could feel the blood rise in her neck. 'Sorry, I shouldn't have said that.' When she opened her eyes, it was only to stare at the floor.

'Please Carla. Don't beat about the bush.' Peppino was struggling to get the words out and laugh at the same time. 'Say what you think, why don't you?'

'Sorry.'

'Oh, don't apologise Carla, it's the best laugh I've had in ages. Now tell me more. I take it, its young Harry you're talking about.' Peppino had calmed down, but a mischievous grin remained.

'It's not funny, he's making so many mistakes, I don't think he really understands the business. He doesn't have a feel for it.'

'If this is because he is not Italian, then let me tell you Carla, neither are you. Go back to Barga and they will soon let you know. Carmela married a Scotsman, but your cousins had the same upbringing as you and your brothers. You are all Scots Italian.'

'It's not that Pepino. Carmela wanted Harry to take over. Everyone just went along with it.'

'And you think it should have been you?'

'I could hardly do any worse. Turnover is down. In half the locations we are being hammered by the competition. We will end up closing those sites. We are about to post a loss for the first time in thirty years. It is all since Harry took over.'

Peppino nodded his head, clasped his hands in front of him, and took a few moments to assemble his thoughts.

'Carla, no business has a right to be successful for ever. Your family has had a good run. For more than forty years, only success, save for a few minor setbacks. Your generation has only known good times.' Peppino hesitated. When he continued his voice had softened. 'Could it be you have all grown a little complacent.' Another pause, another softening of tone. 'A little bit lazy perhaps.'

'I'm working sixty hours a week, most of us are. Even Harry puts in the hours. I can't hold that against him.'

'Going through the motions maybe.' Carla looked angry but said nothing. 'I don't mean to be critical. Sometimes all you can do is go through the motions. Like a football manager, whose players are getting old and jaded, but there is no money in the kitty to buy replacements.'

'The problem with Harry is that people just don't seem to like him. He has fallen out with so many people since taking over. Customers, staff, suppliers. He seems to rub them up the wrong way for some reason. He tries so hard to please everybody but ends up pleasing no one.'

Peppino nodded once more and took in a long breath. 'It's that third-generation thing, I'm afraid. It would be no different for you. There is not the same respect for the third generation. All people see is that it was handed to them on a plate. In this case a big giant pizza plate. Okay, there is little good will towards Harry, but why should there be? Harry didn't have a great business idea. Harry didn't get that idea off the ground. Harry didn't risk everything in pursuit of what he believed in. Did he? Why would anyone put themselves out to help him succeed? Believe me Carla it would be the same for you, or your brothers, or any of the other cousins. Nobody loves the third generation, it just all looks too easy for them. Nobody thinks they deserve any success.'

'What you're saying is we are screwed, no matter what we try.'

'No, failure is not inevitable. All I'm saying is it will be difficult to maintain the same level of success the family has enjoyed in the past. A lot will depend on your competition.

How hungry are they to take your place? Have they got the ability to seize this opportunity?

If the new generation has some setbacks but overcome them. If they are all as determined as Tony was and can demonstrate that they really believe in what they are doing. Perhaps then they will gain some respect and the business can climb back to where it once was, but it will take time, and it won't be easy.'

'We must lower our expectations. That's what you are saying, isn't it?'

'The wave that carried Gino and Carmela is petering out, Carla. All the family can do is make sure they are ready for the next one.'

'And if we fail to catch the next wave?'

'Well, there is always ice cream or chips!'

Handyman

by Palma McKeown

When it came to do-it-yourself
dad was very skilled
at getting mum to do it herself
until one day she'd had enough -
he would paint their bedroom.

I was removed to the seaside
for the afternoon
but Troon couldn't compare
with the scene I left behind -
dad, perched on a ladder, so high up
that he could reach out and touch
the tenement ceiling where only
angels and spiders had gone before.

On the seafront they bought me
a small brick of yellow ice cream.
Slotted into a wafer cone
it became my paint brush -
waving it through the air

I coloured in the clouds,
added seagull squiggles
until my ice cream fell to the pavement,
sizzled to a creamy yellow pool.

Back home at last
I ran to the bedroom to find
pools of ice cream everywhere.
Dad lay in bed, six stitches
holding together the gash on his shin.
That wound became his Badge of Courage,
proof, visible at the hoist of a trouser leg,
that he had seen action on the home front.
Having been decorated,
dad never painted again.

Kissing Bridges

By Barney MacFarlane

Modest Beresford O'Shaughnessy: not a typical name for a chap of Glaswegian working class extraction. Yet it made a certain sense. O'Shaughnessy, common enough in those parts where a huge influx of Catholics had fled the blighted mother Ireland — and Donegal, in particular, for Glasgow — and remained, if not rested, in the West of Scotland, begetting in their sad-mouthed wake generations of often similarly afflicted souls, ready at the drop of a perception to wage conflict with the progeny of those escapees from the Ulster provinces of that same, small, angry island who had also ventured to Scotland in search of … not peace, exactly.

Well, he remembered, young Modest, the jumbled brogue of his father and other Irish topers at Neeson's Bar, across the street from their flat, from where the eldest son had been often dispatched in the early 1960s by a fraught mother, fashioned pernicious to the level of cliché by lack of sustenance both physical and psychological and the weight of too many children. Paddy Neeson's stood garish and victorian in Allison Street in the Govanhill district south of the River Clyde where the Irish and the Jews vied for the little comfort there remained to be wrung from the neck of their unforgiving host, Glasgow. The Irish — the men, at least — derived that comfort made liquid flesh in the form of stout ale in bars the like of Neeson's and of which there was no noticeable lack.

"Arrah, ye little shite that ye are," the more than likely riposte to the son's quivering facial muscles as he meekly pressed the swing door a foot or two to inquire after his father. "What class of nerve d'ye have there to think ye might come and fetch your ould da' from the one bit of pleasure that he has?" The next sound invariably a slap, accompanied by resounding approbation from the man's companions, fearful that they too might be summoned similarly at any moment.

Modest then, when his father wasn't breathing in fumes of hot tar in his sometime capacity as a 'lump' labourer on the roads or building sites, or, indeed, gulping the other dark stuff, he was a great fan of Tchaikovsky. Never one for the commonplace, his auld da', Phelim Noel Anthony O'Shaughnessy, reckoned the first name of the great Russian, Piotr – Peter, even – a little on the dull side, despite its Roman Catholic provenance, and much preferred that bestowed on the composer's brother, namely Modest. A bonus, the father reasoned, that it was self-effacing and "not showy at all". Though that sentiment – the usage of such a first name in a poor, working-class district of Glasgow – might be described as debatable. And the fact that a supposedly knowledgeable chum informed Phelim later that both Tchaikovsky siblings were a touch on the "sensitive" side, only served to convince the father that he had been right all along about young Mod, as his son was then called by his pals.

"Aye, but, ma auntie's family. She merrit a Beresford, Uncle Willie, it wis."

"Oh aye," said Peggy, dragging her pal back to reality. "Well, c'moan, we've goat tae get hame soon so's we can get tae the dancin' the night, eh? Let's dangle."

And the Beresford Hotel came to mean much to Rita over the next few years, convinced as she was that she was in some way related to its owner and architect, one William Beresford Inglis.

As the Second World War spread its terror among the citizens, alternatives were desperately sought after. Rita and Peggy found some solace both in the cocktail bar and later in more than one of the bedrooms at the Beresford which had become a favourite spot for American servicemen after 1942, given that its art deco style and its nickname as Glasgow's first skyscraper reminded so many of them of Hollywood movies – and home.

At the end of the war, one of these "Yankee sweethearts" as she and Peggy dubbed them, got Rita pregnant. Stern stuff he may have been made of in wartime, but "Beresford Bobby" as she often whispered in his willing ear, did not have the stomach for fatherhood.

Lucky then, she thought herself at the time when she met Phelim, not long in town and a bit of the bumpkin about his personality, though his smile was dazzling. Rita, if she hadn't known it already, discovered through the long days and years that poverty allied to strong drink were seldom allied to a happy marriage. But marry her he did, not believing his luck that the 'gurls' of this huge city would allow young Irishmen such as himself the pleasure of their company and a little more besides. He was honour-bound, of course, when Rita found herself with child, soon after their very first knee-trembler in Bath Lane following a few drinks in a city centre bar. Just his luck right enough, thought Phelim, but nothing would do but he'd marry the girl. Sure, and what else was there to do, a decent Catholic girl that she was?

Honour-bound he may have been, but a sap for all that, believing as gospel her story that the birth was premature by three months, despite the evidence to the contrary of a fat eight and a half pounds baby boy.

"Would it be fine at all if we called him Modest?" Phelim put it to his new wife.

Surprised as she was by the choice of name, Rita was so relieved to have a father for the baby that she was happy to agree.

And Beresford: well, it was a more circuitous route which led to the middle name. Mod's ma Rita, a poor, bedraggled woman who counted down the hours until bedtime, so that she might have something to look forward to, had also bethought herself, in the deep past at least, a faintly clever individual. Growing up in the aftermath of the Great War, as her family alluded to it, Rita's own mother often recalled some distant memory, wherein a great aunt had married a joiner, who had made a fortune making small wooden, clinker-built pleasure craft of a fine quality, that the toffs liked to show off in a far-off place known as the "Coat Dashoor" in the south of France. The great man, Uncle Willie, as he was referred to in whispering reverence, had bought up a grand pile among nine hundred acres in the Ayrshire countryside with a river, the Stancha, coursing through it. Auntie Mamie, his wife, had the bright idea to call her husband's boats, Stancha Craft, and so discovered before many, apparently brighter others the value of branding.

The Beresfords, Uncle Willie and Auntie Mamie and their four sons who carried on the family business, were held up as a living legend to the poorer members of the extended family ... the scruff, to which Mod's ma belonged, and despite the Beresfords, never, to anyone's certain knowledge, putting a hand in a full pocket to help out any of their relations, they were always regarded as one might the king.

Beresford therefore was a name that meant something and one day, in 1938, when Rita and her chum Peggy were swanning arm in arm along Sauchiehall Street, their hair tied and clamped fast, beneath checked woollen head squares, with a big knot like a bull's testicle at their brows, and their high heels clacking on the pavement, that name appeared before her in huge and modern form.She yanked Peggy to a halt so that they might watch as workmen, with a crane, heaved the sign on to the portico of a new, beautifully curved hotel that was just about to open there. The sign, in its ultra-modern typeface spelled BERESFORD. Rita swooned. Peggy had to grip her friend by the elbow to keep her vertical.

"Christ, Ri-a," (the glottal stop of the Glasgow accent in full flow) "whi-'s the ma-er wi' ye'?"

Rita felt unable to answer at once. After a few gasps she replied, "It's the name ... Beresford. It's oor family name."

"But yer name's McGinley, ya stumer," Peggy added truthfully.

And so Phelim, worn down by the glass paper of existence, turned into a virtual caricature of the Irish drinking man, as he saw what he believed was his son grow distant, while affecting little interest in him or, indeed, affection for him, those emotions only adding to his recourse to maudlin self-justification and or pity which he found consistently attending him in the murk of his stout.

'Deception' then, as opposed to all the other fine names chosen, might have been more suitable for their first-born.

Yet despite the unexplained rupture between father and supposed son, both remained in ignorance of the lie on which the marriage of Phelim O'Shaughnessy and Margarita (pined-for Beresford) McGinley was founded and subsequently foundered.

In the mid-1960s Modest had reduced his name to Mod, lending him, as he saw it, some finesse among his fellow scruff in Govanhill as the older boys backcombed their hair, donned faux fur-trimmed parkas, and bought – or stole – Lambretta and Vespa motor scooters.

Yet Mod was indeed a sensitive soul, though not in the way his father assumed – we shall call Phelim 'father' as no one was any the wiser, apart from Rita, who never let on. Phelim believed Modest to be sensitive in the way that certain individuals would frequent pubs such as the Vintners in Clyde Street on the north bank of the river, and where these certain individuals would indulge in behaviour, the like of which Phelim and his drinking chums would denounce as degenerate. And to make it worse, this web of sin sat just a few hundred yards west of the Roman Catholic cathedral. How could those sinners walk past such hallowed ground, Phelim wondered. "Lord, let them hang their heads for the shame that's in it." He would mutter conspiratorially to his pals at Paddy Neeson's.

For his part, Mod, burying his thoughts in poetry and architecture, had no longing for a sexual relationship with any other than that from the female persuasion – and one member in particular.

Clyde Street, though, and its bridges, particularly the suspension bridge, connecting it with the other side of the broad river, did hold an extraordinary fascination for him. And, of course, that ultimate escape conduit: the sea, symbolised by a 19th century clipper, the SV Carrick, which lay berthed in the river off Clyde Street and was subsequently used as a floating club by the Royal Navy Volunteer Reserve.

At first, when he began to think about them, those bridges symbolised for him one thing in particular – the prospect of escape. Yet the more he considered this theory, he concluded that the symbolism of escape was all that they did, in fact, represent. The reality was more prosaic: for escape, read escapism. Youngsters, sensitive youngsters such as Modest Beresford O'Shaughnessy, named fancifully after a cultured Russian and a – remote, at best – family link, require escapism, sensing that they cannot quite fit in to the brash jigsaw that is their family and surroundings. Beyond his musings of poetry and engineering, Mod's escapist fancies were plain enough: bridges – and Bridget.

He often wondered if her name had anything to do with his longing for her. Probably. Yet she was quite beautiful in a black-eyelined, beehive hairstyled, skinny-legged sort of way. Catholic, too, which pleased his mother and made his father scratch his head in a puzzled manner. Bridget, too, bucked the trend: the lower Glasgow class as an imbecile, drunken, workshy lump, as it was perceived by those less impoverished, frequently retched a gem from its bile. One such gem was Bridget

MacDonald, at seventeen years, one older than Mod, the funny, dark, thin boy with the huge green eyes who lived with this large family in a grubby tenement on the next street. Being a year older, however, felt like a generation to those suffering in their teens. And being a year older as well as being the girl ... well, that was a plain no-no.

So, how to go about wooing Bridget took up Modest's vivid imagination, even when he was pretending to indulge in reading poetry.

"You reading poetry again, useless bugger that you are!" ranted his father on discovering Modest lying stomach-prone on his bed, one of two in the bedroom he shared with his three brothers. "Can you not go out and find a girlfriend like anybody normal?"

Mod disdained to look in the man's direction but smelled the alcohol on his spiteful breath. He also disdained to answer, pondering if there was a trace of irony in the epithet "bugger". Probably not even irony, more like plain speaking. A slap on the back of his head, with a rolled-up copy of the Evening Citizen, was Phelim's rejoinder. Then, thankfully, his exit, leaving Mod to consider the Bridget possibilities. He could ...

a/ Ask her out again. Except she had already laughed in his face when he tried that approach a few weeks earlier. "Whit, go oot wi' you? A child? Ur ye daft?" A child then – that was how she saw him. Think again.

b/ Find out where she went dancing with her mates then put on the irresistible swagger. Mmm ...

c/ Be yourself and appeal to her better nature that despite the "huge age difference", as Bridget had so pointedly put it, they were both cast from the same mould.

After some days agonising over his plan of action, Mod rejected the first course. He then discovered that Bridget and her chums favoured the Lindella, a loud, brash dance spot at the foot of Union Street in the city centre; Mod had never been but was prepared to try it, given that it was favoured by the 'mods'. Try as he did, however, he and two of his pals did not get past the door. "Yese ur too young, boays," rasped the gigantic doorman, shoving them away. "Come back when yese ur oota nappies."

Despite Bridget's own tender years, it was a given that girls always had a better chance of entry, their short-skirted charms an attraction for the bouncers.

That left Modest with one plan and, though it seemed the best from a philosophical point of view, its execution was problematical, the main problem being that, to solve it, he would have to resort at least in some way to 'Plan A'. In other words, approaching her and making his wishes – longings – known to her. This involved what would now be called stalking, but in the relatively innocent 1960s, it meant following Bridget around a little when she was on her own. Mod attempted to do this over the next few days, holding back several yards behind, while the girl went about her daily business: going to school, getting shopping, taking her little brother to the local swimming baths at Calder Street. Try as he might, however, it seemed that Mod might never manage to catch her alone, gregarious person that she was. Then, in the best traditions of sloppy, sentimental literature, the opportunity arose. And a bridge figured in it.

It was a decent day for autumn in that it wasn't pouring. Modest, exiting from a shop in the busy thoroughfare of Victoria Road, saw Bridget walking briskly towards town. His spirits rose: going into town equated with excitement and seeing Bridget alone was so unexpected that he was sure something must come of it. He quickened his pace as he followed her and as she stepped on the arched bridge on the way over the Clyde, he was within a few yards of her. She turned, sensing him behind her.

"Are you following me by any chance?"
"Well …"

"I take it that means yes."

He noticed that her way of speaking was markedly less vulgar than when she was surrounded by her chums. Modest liked that; he often practised speaking 'proper' while standing before the long wardrobe mirror in the communal bedroom, much to the scoffing derision of his siblings if they walked in on him.

Caught in the act once more, Modest tried a different tack. "It's not often that a beautiful girl takes a walk over this bridge."

Was that a hint of pink on her cheek? If so, she bowed her head a little so that she might prevent him from seeing it. "OK then, flatterer, what's so special about this bridge then?"

He was thinking on his feet now, yet buoyed with some confidence, not least as she deigned to speak to him. Smiling, he replied, "Nothing special really. It's just that people usually take the bus."

That was it: the icebreaker. She laughed. Mod had heard that when you got a girl to laugh then the next bit was easy. They stopped and stood together, gazing across the river, straining their eyes to see the docks in the far distance. "So, tell me about this bridge then, Smarty pants. I bet you don't know anything about it."

But in that, Bridget was wrong. Mod knew all right.

"Albert Bridge. Built in 1841 by Bell and Miller. Named after Prince Albert." And pointing to a nearby crest, added, "Look, that's his coat of arms."

"Mm, really? And what's so good about it that you know all about it?"

Mod smiled again; she seemed to like it. He wondered if he should press his luck. "Well, I like to think of it as a kissing bridge."

"What, you mean you bring girls here and kiss them?"

"Well, I haven't done it so far but then I haven't met anyone as beautiful as you before."

"Ah, go on with you. You're just a chancer."

She did allow herself to be kissed, however. And she would always remember all the details she learned that day, about Albert Bridge in particular and kissing bridges in general, such as the tiny 'romantic' example at the boating lake in Victoria Park in the west end of the city, where Mod and Bridget visited occasionally. And even the Pont Neuf in Paris, the so-called 'king of bridges', where Modest – his first name did not sound at all out of place in that city – and by now, Brigitte found their way by degrees.

The pitch and toss blare of the ambulance alarm was familiar to Modest finally, as he weaved in and out of consciousness, heading to who knew what fate. Despite his fragile condition, he sensed – knew, even – that all the memories of a life, however capacious, were capable of distilling into a few moments when the need arose. He knew the year was now 2009; he knew his mind had swept forward at speed from the late 1950s, yet he had no sensation of speed, only that, in his perilous state, the story of his life was forcing itself to be remembered, not to the world, but merely to him, an audience of one and the only one who mattered. The only one left.

For Modest knew tragedy. He was acquainted with grief, as Isaiah put it, though not despised, and rejected of men. Throughout his humble beginnings then fabulous, and happily childless, life with Brigitte in their respective roles as architect and art critic, intellectual and cultural denizens of their adopted city of Paris, and feted for their wit and sensitivity, Modest, to his cost, was acquainted with the sound of a siren.

The first occasion was certainly the most dramatic, containing both police and ambulance vehicles, though it had less of a lasting effect on him. A year into his relationship with Bridget, he was seventeen when his youngest sibling, Maria, then aged eight, tumbled through an open window to her death on an unforgiving pavement, thirty feet below, during an unusually warm afternoon in August. It was just one day before she was due to return to school, after the silence over the circumstances of her firstborn's entry into the world.

Even then, however, Rita could not bring herself to wring the truth from her conscience, and took the secret of Modest to her grave, which occurred just one month later, thanks to a cocktail of paracetamol and cheap wine – Lanliq. As her son holidayed, she spent long weeks attempting to amuse several young children, while worrying about money and an errant husband who preferred stout to family. It had taken their toll on her. Rita, in a constant sweat about how she might resolve all the wrongs in her life, had thrown open the windows to their top floor flat, in the hope of some respite from the rising levels of humidity. She might have repented at leisure, but for the fact that she saw little Maria's death as a debt for her recalled, while his own emergency transport now hurtled through the Parisian boulevards.

The second ambulance siren, Modest remembered, came six months later as the vehicle pulled up sharply outside Paddy Neeson's bar, inside which Phelim O'Shaughnessy, more sinning than sinned against, had suffered what turned out to be a fatal heart attack. Modest had been making the evening meal for his remaining siblings – three brothers aged from ten to fifteen and two sisters aged thirteen and nine. The familiar noise had roused them and brought Modest to the window. From this vantage point he saw the emergency team stretcher his father, his skin the colour of old newspaper, beneath an oxygen mask, into the back of the ambulance. He felt no shock, no sadness either, only relief. He sensed that by the time the ambulance got to the nearby Victoria Infirmary, his father would be dead. In that, Modest was proved correct.

The local newspapers made much of the tragedies to befall the O'Shaughnessy family; one even spoke of a curse. Yet

Modest knew that if there were a curse it was a twin variety visited upon them by their father and strong drink.

Within a few months, the family had been sundered. The next casualty was Gerard, second in line to Modest whose younger siblings had been bestowed with 'normal' names, given that his parents believed they had made a grave mistake in their naming of the eldest. Gerard, wayward even for the picaresque surroundings of Govanhill, landed in a List D school – later jail, having failed to go straight – following his arrest for housebreaking. An aunt, the elder sister of Rita, took in the two remaining little sisters – "Ah'm no' huvin' any boays. Nothin' but trouble, so they are," she announced, perfectly reasonably.

Which left a few years in a children's home for the other two brothers.

Modest's next step could not have been more removed from the fate of his siblings if he had engineered it. One year earlier, his girlfriend Bridget had won a place at Chelsea College of Art and now Modest had been accepted to attend University College London to study architecture. He could join her at last. The imbalance of his family's circumstances was not lost on him, yet he treasured the idea that he might fulfil his ambition: one day he would step on that mythical bridge and walk right out of Glasgow. Which he did, crossing many bridges along the way, not least Chelsea Suspension Bridge, on which he and Bridget often kissed as they strolled across to Battersea Park and its riotous funfair, pretend-choking on the smoke from the four chimneys of Battersea Power Station to their left.

Over the years, he experienced mixed fortune as he attempted to help his brothers and sisters. During holidays, he and Bridget visited Gerard in Barlinnie prison, but despite Modest's encouragement to "straighten yourself out", the younger brother revelled in his crimes and concomitant, though merely occasional, wealth.

The girls, given a home by their aunt and taken on holiday with Modest and Bridget when they could afford it, fared well enough in the milieu of 1980s Glasgow, one becoming a hairdresser and marrying a decent bloke, the other ending up a nursing sister in the very hospital where her mother, father, and baby sister all perished.

Life for the two boys in care was more difficult. Modest visited them too, in the children's home in the Maryhill district where they lived. One, encouraged eventually by one of the teachers, became a research chemist, specialising in the principles of bonding: chemical, not human, yet the latter sort fascinated him eventually, too. But the other ended up a heroin addict – the ambulance siren beckoning once more.

That jarring noise did not stop for Modest. Even now, as he supposed his carriage must be approaching the hospital, the pains in his chest refusing to recede, he remembered the last time he had heard it. But then as he did so, another vision appeared in his mind. It was like a dream, the way the thoughts fought each other for prominence. He knew it must have been less than an hour since he had collapsed at his desk, yet the memories flitted in and out like a newsreel. And then an image he cherished: a scene from David Lean's movie Brief Encounter where to the strains of the Rach 2, Laura and Alec, walking after their last drive to the country, had strolled on to an ancient hump-backed bridge.

"Look, darling, a kissing bridge!" Brigitte, as she had become, enthused, as she and Modest watched the film years earlier, on the sofa in their Montparnasse apartment, their first together in Paris.

A kissing bridge indeed. As all bridges had become for Modest and Brigitte.

He had watched the movie again just the previous week on television. And wept. Wept for his poor darling who had wasted away three years ago, yet when her final moments came, it was the ambulance siren again to the fore as it swept her, pointlessly, to hospital.

His heart now weakening by the minute, he succumbed to what he believed was the genetic legacy, endowed by his drunken father.

And so, it was now: the siren, that siren which had fashioned his life in so many awful ways which now rang out a different call. As he felt the strength drain from his body, Modest Beresford O'Shaughnessy gave thanks for the sound. Having spurned religion as a young man, the siren nevertheless sounded … well, heavenly.

And beckoning…

Over bridges.

Kissing his beloved Brigitte.

"I'm coming, darling."

Laundry Lady

by Marco Giannasi

Every garment has its history,

every stain is a reminder,

every scent a souvenir.

The shorts belonging to the small boy

who landed in a puddle of dirty water

and was scolded by his mother.

The soldier's uniform stained

with the warm blood of a stranger

who died for nothing.

That woman's apron, splashed

with a tomato sauce so delicious

that he couldn't bear to leave her.

The nightdress soaked in sweat

and the forbidden perfume

of a moment's madness.

The sweater covered in grass,

dried earth and small flowers
that acted as a blanket.

Lipstick from those lips,
imprinted on that shirt
like sin's own seal.

The missing button, wrenched
off in a moment
of wrongful forced violence.

The towel used to dry
delicately and sensually
that sweet, innocent skin.

The first baby gown worn
by a new arrival in this world,
full of joy and life.

The last garment worn
for the final time
before I depart.

LONDON FOR A TENNER: 1980
By Alex Meikle

As he alighted from the bus in the shabby surroundings of Victoria Coach Station, Aiden felt the fresh air hit him with relief. Somewhere on the M1, a couple of hours back, the air conditioning had failed, plunging the coach in sweltering heat during a UK wide heatwave. The driver had given his passengers a blunt alternative. He could either pull into the first service station, report the defect, and wait possibly hours for a replacement, or sweat it out and press on to London. The option to continue was unanimous.

Aiden retrieved his large brown case, which the driver had extracted from the luggage hold and placed it on the tarmac, beside the coach. As he lifted it, he groaned at the weight of the case and silently cursed his mother. He was only away for a long weekend in London, another ten days in Amsterdam, and if the money lasted, a few more in Hamburg. But she'd packed the case the previous evening with every conceivable item of clothing, as if he'd be gone for months.

He lugged the case through the station out onto Buckingham Palace Road. The relief he felt hitting the fresh air, on exiting the coach, after seven hours travelling from Glasgow, rapidly dispersed. Late afternoon, central London in early August, was stiflingly hot with a cloudless sky and not a breath of wind in the air. Aiden crossed the busy road and followed the blond Portland stone west wall of Victoria Railway station. He was making for the main entrance where, in about an hour's time, he'd meet his friend, Kenny, probably have a few beers and then go back to Kenny's digs somewhere up in North London just off the quaintly named Seven Sisters Road.

Kenny and he had been electrical engineering students at Strathclyde University, but Kenny had dropped out after first year and had moved to London to chance his luck. He now worked as a security guard, patrolling a construction site in Hounslow in the far west of the city, and he was on dayshift this Saturday. His shift finished at six and he was due to meet Aiden at the station entrance shortly after. Aiden would spend the next few days with Kenny, until heading over to Amsterdam, where his cousin rented a flat which he shared with his Dutch girlfriend. Both worked in a factory sorting tulip bulbs.

At last, he reached the entrance to the station. He checked his watch; it was only after five: the coach had got in early. He had an hour to wait for Kenny. There were some benches outside the entrance where he could sit and wait for him, but what really drew his attention was a pub across the way named the *Chaucer Arms*. He was hot, sweaty, and above all dehydrated and choking for a pint. After resting for a few minutes, he headed across to the pub.

Outside the pub there were dozens of football fans, dressed in bright red and white supporter's strips or bearing scarves or rosettes with the same colours, all drinking pints, some chanting, all quite gregarious. Aiden assumed by their happy demeanour they'd beaten their opponents that afternoon. Dragging his case, which he now hated with a vengeance, he arrived at the main entrance. But he quickly realised, there was a problem. The inside of the pub was absolutely stowed with supporters. From what he could see through the open doors, every available space was taken. Trying to get through on his own would be a struggle. Lugging a bloody great suitcase through that mob would be well-nigh impossible.

He sat forlornly on the case in front of the pub, hoping that a few customers would leave and allow some space. But after five long minutes not a soul had left. He was about to give up and go back to the benches outside the station, when he noticed a guy coming round the corner of the pub, collecting empty glasses. He was small and wiry with medium length brown hair, wearing a grey sweater, and a cloth draped over one shoulder. The guy began collecting empty glasses, folk had left on the ledges or near the edge of the pub, while engaging in banter with the punters. He was obviously staff, and an idea came to Aiden.

'Excuse me, mate,' Aiden called him over. The guy was wearing a broad grin as he approached him.

'I don't think I'm going to win a Nobel Prize for working out what you want guvnor?'

His smile was infectious, and Aiden returned the smile and relaxed, next to the case, as the guy went on:

'You're looking for a pint? That's ok, what you looking for?'

'Aw, you're a godsend, pal. I could murder a pint of bitter.'

'Consider it done. Where you travelled from?'

'Glasgow. Seven bloody hours on a coach, the last three without air conditioning.'

'Jesus, mate, you certainly deserve a beer. Where are you off to?'

'Amsterdam, then maybe Germany, just for a couple of weeks.'

'Well, you've come well prepared,' the guy said pointing to the heavy case.

'It's my bloody mother,' Aiden sighed. 'I let her do my packing for me and she's left me with this. I've seen guys going halfway round the world for months travelling lighter than this!'

The guy let out a short laugh. 'That's mothers for you. They always think you're about nine years old. Anyway, I better get that pint before you die of thirst.'

But the guy made no move to go into the pub and an awkward silence descended, before the barman eventually said with an air of embarrassment:

'Sorry mate, but we're in the west end. If I go back in there, pour you a pint in front of at least a dozen thirsty customers who've waited ages, then bring that pint out and,' he raised his free hands 'now don't take this the wrong way, but you grab that pint off me, neck it in a oner and do a runner and I go back empty handed, my gaffer will hang, draw and quarter me.'

Aiden protested vigorously: 'But I would never do that, I…'

'…Now, I didn't say you would, mate,' the guy interrupted. 'But it's been done before.' Suddenly, the guy looked away from Aiden, stared into the crowded bar and shouted to someone inside: 'Davy, for God's sake collect those empties from round the other side, they're getting slaughtered and running out of glasses at the bar!' He turned back to Aiden. 'Sorry, mate, I need to get in there,' he made towards the pub entrance.

'Hold on!' Aiden cried. He fetched out his brown leather wallet, his mother had bought him for Christmas, and withdrew a fresh Bank of England ten-pound note, which he'd obtained from his bank yesterday, as he didn't want to endure any hassle with Scottish notes, when in England. 'Here pal, pint of bitter please,' he said almost pleadingly and proffered the barman his note.

'I'll be as quick as I can guv, there'll be a backlog of these to get through,' he said, taking the note from Aiden with one hand, while indicating the pile of glasses, he was clutching hold of with his other hand and arm.

Aiden sat back on his case feeling relieved. He could see the barman's point though. The staff here must have seen every trick in the book, including the one the barman had graphically highlighted. Relaxing now, he looked at his watch. There was still another fifty minutes before Kenny was due to turn up.

He thought of his impending trip to Amsterdam, "the Dam," of coffee shops, hash, late night bars and, perhaps, the red-light district. And, if he eked his money out, there might be space for Hamburg. He'd saved long and hard for this trip despite living on a pittance of a student grant, although, to be fair, his folks had helped him out as well. No, he was certainly looking forward to this break.

After five minutes, he gazed towards the bar. There was no sign of the barman, and it was still mobbed in there. He reflected on what the barman had said to his colleague; they were getting 'slaughtered' in there. Feeling a bit uncomfortable perched on the case, he got up, yawned, and stretched out his arms. As he did so, he heard the heavy sounds of diesel engines approaching and then saw five grey and white coaches drive up outside the Chaucer Arms.

As they parked, their drivers idling their engines, there was movement from both outside and inside the bar, as the away fans gulped down their pints, collected their banners and scarves, and made their way towards the coaches, singing and chanting, some giving Aiden a friendly pat on the back as they went past him. It was like a mass exodus and within minutes the bar had emptied.

Taking hold of his case, Aiden walked into the pub. rays of sunlight penetrating the gloomy interior. It was like the aftermath of a wild party. Foam flecked glasses, many with dregs of beer, were piled everywhere on tables, ledges, even on the floor along with crammed ashtrays and discarded coasters. One barman, Aiden presumed it was 'Davy' was running about collecting glasses, while behind the bar, four staff were furiously washing glasses and wiping the bar down. Aiden could see no sign of his barman and slowly approached the bar with his case.

One of the staff nearest to Aiden, attending to an open till jam packed with notes, became aware of his hovering presence. He gestured towards another member of staff wiping the bar and said:

'Will, get that guy there, could you?' Aiden presumed the guy at the till was the manager.

'It's ok,' he said apologetically, 'I'm getting served.'

The manager looked perplexed. 'Who's serving you?' he asked quizzically, looking around at his staff.

'The guy that was collecting glasses outside.' Aiden looked at the staff but couldn't see his barman amongst them.

'Nobody's been outside mate. We've been hammered in here.'

The guy collecting glasses from the tables deposited some of them at the bar beside Aiden.

'You Davy?' Aiden asked.

'No guv, I'm Arnie.' The guy went back to collecting glasses. Confused, Aiden asked: 'You've got a Davy working here?'

The manager shook his head. 'No, pal and there's been no one outside. Why?'

Before he answered, Aiden noticed all the staff were wearing maroon-coloured sweatshirts with the legend *Chaucer's*, emblazoned on the front. His "barman" had been wearing a grey jumper.

'I paid a guy outside ten quid for a pint of bitter,' he finally answered pitifully. 'He had a cloth over his shoulder and a pile of glasses in his hand.'

All motion had stopped from the staff behind the bar; the staff's eyes fixed on him. The manager remarked with brutal precision:

'Mate, you've been done. That guy's seen you as a mark. You'll never see that tenner again.'

Aiden finally had to admit he'd been conned. He felt angry and humiliated. He asked:

'Can I get a pint anyway?'

'Sure, but you'll need to pay for it.'

'But I've just walked off the bus and been conned!' He protested.

'Whose fault is that mate? You're in the middle of bleeding London. Always keep your wits about you. Besides, I'm running a business here, not a bloody charity for the easily duped. Now, you want a pint or not?'

Aiden shook his head in frustration. 'Forget it,' he didn't want to stay another second in that pub. Biting back tears, he took his case and walked outside. On the way out, he heard the manager say to his staff in mocking tones:

'Watcher make of that then: "Can I get a free pint?" Honestly!'

Outside, Aiden looked over at the imposing façade and entrance to Victoria station, a frenetic hive of activity even at this time on a Saturday afternoon. Yet again he looked at his watch. There were still forty-five minutes before Kenny was due to show up.

Only thirty bloody minutes in London, he reflected, and he'd been done for a tenner.

HOMEWORK

by Lizzie Allan

Dae ye 'hink ah'm gauni sit 'n dae

'grammar exercises' the night, man?

Dae ye 'hink ah'm gauni get that mad *essay* 'hing

finished the night?

Ah've goat better 'hings tae dae wae ma time!

Ah canny dae it - 'cos ah've

goat tae go oot the night.

Ah'm playin' fitbaw wi' the guys 'n that.

Ah dae that *every* night.

Yir worried aboot mi?

Whit ur YOU worried aboot ME fur?

Ah'm no worried!

Ah've goat a job set up fur mi

in ma uncle's windae business.

The noo.

Fur life!

Ah would leave here the morra if ah could.

Get away fae aw this *solid* stuff, man –

'n away fae YOU n'aw!

How did ye wahnt tae be a English teacher?

Did ye wahnt tae be wan aw yer life?

Well ….ah'd *never* dae that!

Spend yer life moanin' 'n naggin'…

Fur whit?

Naw.

Efter the fitbaw, ah'll be gaun doon

the back ae the library
tae huv a wee swally 'n a wee smoke –
meet up wae the pals 'n that.
'N ah think there's gauni be a fight
doon the park......

Magic, man! Ah canny wait!

It's gauni be a boatle fight.
Last time, ah goat cracked 'n the heid!
Then - when it wis dun -
we flung wur boatle taps at the trees.
Ye ought tae ah seen the doos scarper!

Then wi flung wur empty cans
intae a wumman's beau-i-ful gerdin
'n she stuck 'er heid oot the windae
'n telt us she wis gauni phone the polis.
Man – that wis dead funny –
'er heid wis tight wae wee rollers.
Then 'er cat flew oot the windae .
Wheeeecht!
'N away it shot – like a bullit through butter!

Naw.

Ah huvny goat time tae dae
aw that *'homework'* stuff the night, Miss –

Ah've goat mair important 'hings tae dae..........

64

Heller's Lift

By Ian Goudie

'You could try to be a little more enthusiastic.'

'I know, Margaret, but...'

'But what, Thomas? This place has got everything that we have ever wanted. There is even an indoor toilet. You know how much you hate shuffling down the close and out to the backcourt with that bad leg of yours. Especially after dark - when the nightmares awake you.'

'I know, I know.'

'And there is a bedroom each for little Brian and Christine, a kitchenette, and central heating. Where is that brochure again?'

As Margaret searched her periwinkle leather bag, I took a moment to admire her. She always looked so smart. Today was no exception. Her turquoise suit and sky-blue shoes complimented her angelic eyes. She had recently grown her hair a bit longer, and the black curls framed her beautiful oval face perfectly. There was no doubting it. Margaret was a looker; no wonder all my mates were jealous.

'You're punching above your weight,' Auld Boab ad honce said. 'She looks just like the Queen.'

I smiled as I recalled my snappy comeback line, 'Don't you know they're twins? Baith were born on the twenty-first of April 1926. It's just that Elizabeth Regina was born in Mayfair, and Margaret Rae in Maryhill.'

I guess I'd always known that Margaret and I would get married, even when I was just a wee lad. My family lived at 12 Niven Street. The Raes were just around the corner on Stirrat Street. We both went to Napiershall Street Primary School and then down the road to Woodside Secondary. I can still remember the big school's motto, *Fortitudeine vincemus* - by endurance we conquer. I shake my head at its naivety, wondering what the school founders knew about endurance or conquering.

'Here it is, said Margaret, "Moss Heights has all modern amenities and offers families the opportunity to raise their children in a healthy and safe environment with fresh air, playing fields and panoramic views over Pollok Country Park." What is not to like?'

'But, Doll, it's oan the ninth flair! How am I supposed to climb up a' those stairs wi' ma gammy leg?'

'Oh Thomas, don't be so silly. There's a lift.'

'Aye, well I'll no' be taking it. Look at it, it's tiny!'

'Thomas!'

'I'd raither use the stairs, even wi' ma bad leg.'

'You will not. You will get in this lift. Now!'

I take a long drag of my Woodbine fag, savouring the impact of the nicotine as it reaches my lungs. Leaning back, I slowly exhale the blue smoke which floats gently along the tiled hallway towards the exit. Suddenly, I feel a sharp pain in my leg. A grimace spreads across my face.

'What is it, Thomas? What is wrong?' asked Margaret.

'It's nowt.'

'Are you sure?'

'I'm a' right,' I mumbled.

'What did you mean earlier when you said the lift was tiny? It is not that small.'

'A didnae mean anything. Honest, it's nowt.'

'You can speak to me, Thomas. You do know that don't you? You are never shy when talking about your work. Always telling me just how bad the management is at the shipyard. 'Donkeys leading lions,' you call them. You are so forthright when talking about the problems your workmates have, but when it comes to talking about yourself you always clam up like a shell. You know, you have never even told me what happened to your injured leg.'

'Margaret, can you just droap it?'

'It has been nine years since the war ended. Things have changed a lot in that time. You have changed a lot, Thomas Heller. You have worked hard and studied hard too. Few people realise just how difficult it was for you, with your poor concentration, but you did it. I am so proud of you. All those evenings not going out for a drink and a laugh with the rest of the Maryhill lads. Instead, you chose to invest in our future by going to the Royal Technical College and achieving your City and Guilds. The girls used to tease me about going out with a 'college boy'. But look at us now, Thomas. You, a draughtsman at Harland and Wolff's Fairfield yard, and a shop steward too. And me, the proud mother of two gorgeous children. Brian is almost eight years old now. He has started asking why his father can't play football with him. He wants to know what happened to your leg, Thomas, and so do I.'

I stayed silent for a moment or two, trying to get my brain cells into working gear. She was right, our mates had slagged me for being boring and going to college. God knows we all needed some fun after the horrors of the war. But they were all single, whilst I had a wife to support. I was the first male in my family ever to go to college, but I was not the first in my family. That honour goes to Margaret. When I was away learning how to be a soldier. – bored to tears with all that marching, cleaning my rifle, and bulling my boots - she had spent three months at college, training to be an electrician. She even worked in Fairfield's before me.

Every morning she would don her baggy blue boilersuit and carefully climb down narrow metal ladders, with one hand carrying her toolbox, into the bowels of the ship. Where she would spend all day installing electrical cables in the sailors' cabins. She was so good at her job, that they transferred her to John Brown's in Clydebank to work on HMS Vanguard. At the time, the biggest and fastest Royal Navy battleship ever built. Two of Margaret's colleagues lost their lives, and six others were injured when a blinding explosion ripped the ship during its fitting-out. But Margaret was never feart. And here's me, the 'man of the hoose', too scared to enter a silly wee lift.

I know more about her wartime experiences than she knows of mine. Old soldiers don't talk about what happened during their wars, apart from the likes of Blunden and Sassoon. Posh poets from Oxford and Cambridge Universities who had fought in World War 1. But what good had talking and writing about their experiences done them? None. Even now, more than thirty-five years later, they were still suffering from their war. Hearing the voices of soldiers singing, shouting, and screaming, and smelling the deadly stench of trenches and battlefields. No, talking about what happened in wars never helped anyone.

I took another draw on my cigarette. Coughing as the tobacco smoke reached the back of my dry throat, then with my eyes rigidly fixed on the steel floor, avoiding Margarets' gaze, I replied hesitantly,

'Aye...you're right. Nine years is a long time. Nine years since I came hame fae Burma. I can still see the faces of those waiting for us; proudly waving their Union Jacks in the rain as their sons and husbands marched doon frae the ships docked oan the Clyde. Ma mither and you waiting patiently for me, wondering where a wis. Until you spotted them pushing me doon the gangway in a bloody wheelchair, wi the rest of the war-wounded. Whit a sight we must have been. Wrapped in blood-stained bandages. Some managed to keep upright aided by cheap canes and crutches and hobbled and waddled along, whilst me and the others were wheeled aff the ship by nurses and comrades. The wounded, the maimed, the blind and the insane, returning hame to a hero's welcome.

Nine years of limping aboot Glesga wi' a walking stick. Struggling to get up the close stairs. Weans in the street cawing me 'Hopalong Heller.' I dinnae need any mair reminders o' ma bloody sair leg!'

'Now, there's no need to swear, Thomas.'

'Aye, well. I'm sorry, but whit dae ye expect?'

I watched Margaret as she strode confidently to the back of the lift and stood waiting for me. She could have had anyone, but she stuck by me. Maybe we married too young. At seventeen, she was just a lassie working as a shop assistant wi' a heid fu' of romantic dreams. I wis just a raw lad who knew nowt but thought he knew everything. I would have done anything for that bonnie young lassie. When she said that we should get married before the army sent me abroad, I agreed. We didnae have much time. So, we settled for a wee wedding at the registration office. Just immediate family and a couple of friends. It wasn't exactly the 'big day' that she had dreamed of. Of course, she never said anything, but I knew she was worried that something might happen to me. I guess, she was right to worry.

I stood rooted at the lift entrance. I just couldnae move. My eyes darted left, then right. I glanced up, then down. I strained my ears listening for any sound, any warnings. But there was nothing. I rested my sweating left hand on the outside of the lift entrance and took a deep breath. The coldness of the sheet metal ran up my arm and down my leg. My good leg started shaking.

'Thomas, come in here!' Maggie ordered.

'A need...a need the toilet,' I lied, looking over my shoulder.

'I told you, there's one in the flat.'

I lugged my legs just inside the door, squeezing my lumpen body into the left-hand corner of the lift.

'Press the button. Number nine.'

I took one last drag of my Woodbine, exhaled the smoke, and tossed the dowt into the red fire bucket at my feet, before leaning forward and pressing the stupid button. The metal doors slid shut with a short, shrill shriek. Followed by a muffled thud as the two doors met. The last few lingering rays of natural light slunk under the metal doors. The concealed lights above our heads flickered on and the lift groaned into life, like a wounded beast as it jittered from side to side. I heard the ghostly screams of unseen metal cables out as they tightened stiff, and then pulled the lift upward. Sluggishly rising away from the safety of the concrete floor. I clenched my hot fists around the head of my wooden walking cane. The blood in my wrist arteries pulsated like a piston. A long, slow deep breath. Then let it go. Breathe. I whispered the numbers of the floors as their lights lit up as we squealed our way slowly upwards, '1... 2... 3... 4...'

Suddenly, the lift screeched to a halt; the lights went out. I stumbled backwards, banging the back of my head against the hard metal wall. My eyes slammed shut and my fists fell open. I heard the shallow sound of my walking stick bouncing on the floor. Like an echo. Then silence...

My head felt fuzzy like it was full of cotton wool, but then slowly cleared. My eyes blinked open, but it was still dark. There was a strange smell, a sickly stench that reminded me of somewhere from a long time ago. Perhaps football dressing rooms? No, another place. The army.

I coughed. Started to shiver. A layer of sweat formed below my Khaki Drill uniform. I wiped the amber beads from my brow, then moaned, 'Christ, it's hoat in here!'

A loud Cockney voice retorts, 'Of course, it's hot. We're in a Stuart tank in the middle of the Burmese jungle. What the hell do you expect? It's always hot in this tin oven. It was hot yesterday, it's hot today, and I'll bet you a threepenny piece, that tomorrow it will be as hot as Betty Grable. Now, is there anything else, Gunner Heller?'

'Aye, Sergeant.'

'Well. What is it, Heller?'

'A need a shit.'

'It's I need a shit, *sir*.'

'A need a shit, *sir*!'

'Well, use the bucket. What do you want me to do, wipe your *bottle and glass*?'

I loosened my belt, pulled down my trousers, squatted down on the bucket, and groaned through gritted teeth, 'Nnn, nnn, nngg, nnngg.'

'What's that noise?' asked the sergeant.

'It's me, I'm having a shit... *sir*!'

'Quiet. Listen. Can you hear it?'

I whisper, 'What is it, sir?'

'It's the Japs. They're underneath us.'

'Under the tank? For God's sake, whit are they daeing there?'

Sergeant Jones explained how the Japanese soldiers dug spider holes in the path of allied tanks, climbed into them - with two hand grenades and a pistol – and hid below some camouflage. As soon as they sensed an armoured vehicle above them, they pulled the grenade pins - blowing up the tank, and themselves, to smithereens. If they survived the blast, they shot themselves. Sarge said that they admired such behaviour in Japan, 'Death instead of defeat. It's part of their culture, they call it *kamikaze*.'

Suddenly there is a loud bang. The tank staggers to a stop. The smell of bombs and blood fill the air. I feel a sharp pain shooting up my leg and let out a deadly scream, 'Arghhh!'

'Gunner Heller? Are you all right, Heller?'

'It's ma leg, Sergeant. The *kamikaze* Japs have blown up ma bloody leg!'

The lift growls into action, heaving slowly upwards. The lights flicker into life. I see Margaret still standing there in the back of the lift. Her face looks pale. She's looking down at me as if she's not believing what she sees, as if she's waiting for something to change. But it doesn't, it's me, her husband, sitting on a galvanised bucket with ma troosers roon ma ankles and holding onto ma outstretched leg.

'Thomas, what are you doing down there? Has something happened to your bad leg?'

'Has something happened to ma leg? Wumin, can you no' see the blood pouring oot o' it? The Japs have blown a hole in ma left leg. That's whit happened to ma leg.'

The lift screeches and staggers to a halt. The lights go out.

'Gunner Heller are you all right?' asks the sergeant.

'Naw, I'm no. I'm dying.'

'Heller, you are not dying.'

'I'm too young to die!'

'Son, you're not dying; just do exactly as I tell you, and you'll be fine.'

'Fine?! Fine?! Have you seen the blood gushing oot o' ma leg?'

'Pull off your belt. Now, fasten it around your leg, just above the wound.'

I wipe ma nose with the back of ma haun, it smells o' blood. I take a deep breath. Let it out. 'Okay, Sarge.'

'Now, pull that belt as tight as you can, like a poulterer strangling a chicken.'

I'm too weak to argue that I've never seen a poulterer, so I follow my orders, nearly passing out with the pain. My screams bounce off the walls, echoing like cries from the dying doomed. The deathly noise fades. My eyelids close like shop shutters. Darkness.

The sergeant shouts louder, 'Tighter, Heller. Tighter!'

I pull the belt tighter. Pain. Nausea. I feel my face getting hotter, turning red and blotchy, my eyes turning bloodshot. My eyelids spring open and cold tears trickle down my burning face. There's a lump in my throat. My voice cracks as I try to speak. 'Sarge.'

'Hold it there. Jam it tight with your pocketknife. Stick your knife into the buckle.'

I don't know what to do. The pain says, 'Close your eyes and I'll go away.' It sounds so easy. But my army training says, 'Ignore the pain and follow orders.' I do what the Sarge said, stick my knife into the buckle, then slowly release my grip.

The belt stays in place. The improvised tourniquet stems the flow of blood. My head drops back.

'Breathe! Gunner Heller, breathe! That's an order.'

My eyes get heavy; I can't stop them from re-closing. My shoulder crashes against the wall. Darkness. Then I hear her voice, Margaret, saying my name, 'Thomas! Thomas!'

Opening my eyes, I see that she's crouched down beside me. 'Whaur am I? Whit happened?'

'It is all right, Thomas. You gave me such a fright, but I am here. I'm really worried about you. I think you have been hallucinating, having one of your nightmares again. You are getting them more often these days. We need to do something. We both know that we can't continue like this. We are both supposed to be planning for a better future for us and our children, but part of you is still stuck in the past. Half your mind is still busy fighting yesterday's wars. We need to do something. We should have a word with Dr Simpson. We need to talk to someone.'

'A dinnae need to see a doctor. A dinnae need to talk to oanyboady. There's nothing the matter wi' me. I'm okay. I'm no' mad. No, not me. I'm a man, a soldier. I'm Gunner Heller, 7th Armoured Brigade, serial number: 25965701.'

Silence.

Tapping. I hear something tapping beneath the floor.

Margaret says, 'Thank God, here are the firemen.' but I dinnae understaun whit she means. I grab my rifle; sit up straight. Point the barrel to the floor; take aim. A panel drops from the floor; then a head emerges through the gap. A helmet. A uniform. I take aim, but my rifle willnae fire. He climbs inside; sits down beside me. He's grinning. He stairts talking, but his voice is wrang, it's no' Japanese, it's English. He's speaking English, with a Glasgow accent. I'm confused. Whit's happening?

'You're okay, pal. You'll be all right. Here, gie me that walking stick before you hairm someone.'

He takes my rifle and helps me to my feet. I see Margaret watching. Saying nothing. Just standing there looking, as the Jap takes me prisoner.

There is a slight smile on his face as he takes another puff of his pipe, exhales slowly and says, 'We call it Combat Stress Reaction these days. The medical profession has not used the term Shell Shock since 1917. We have a slightly better understanding of what we are dealing with now than we did in those dark ages.' Dr Simpson still has that reassuring voice that he has always had, the one that old doctors have. This is just as well, as I feel stupid sitting on the edge of the white vinyl chair, rocking slightly back and forward, fidgeting, and looking down at the dull grey carpet.

The doc said that thousands of British veterans are still being treated for the illness almost a decade after the war. I wonder how many more there are. Men like me, ex-servicemen living with invisible scars, fighting battles in their brains. Too ashamed to talk. Worried that folk would think that we were soft, cowards even. Anyway, what would happen if they came forward? They'd probably get locked up in loony bins.

'You look worried, Tommy. There's no need to be concerned. The asylums are overflowing as it is with people who need our help, not brave ex-soldiers like you. We have a new medicine from France, chlorpromazine. It's what we call a psychotropic drug, but you don't need to remember that; all you need to do is take two pills three times a day after meals. Will you do that for me? Not just for yourself, but for Margaret and the children? Doctor's orders.'

'Of course, I will. I'm a soldier.'

Love and Wisdom

by Henry Buchanan

"It's impossible to love and be wise,"

Says Shakespeare, so let us his phrase incise:

In love there's laxity and resignation,

Habit, emotional ossification –

Our friend, wisdom, out of the window flies.

So we chuck love to once more wisdom court,

For steady wisdom's bold love never dies.

But, as new wisdom's test is love's strong fort,

Wisdom in abstract void frustrated becomes.

So: in love, out of wisdom (and vice versa):

How then do we stop our two friends' inertia?

How do we fight love and wisdoms' inverse sums?

We two-time in our emotional kingdom –

50% Love, 50% Wisdom!

To Miss X, on her 30th birthday

AREA Z

By Duncan McDonald

Yarrows Naval Shipyard, Clydeside Scotland

Commander Paula Sinclair had just taken delivery of a brand-new submarine built by a consortium of shipyards, led by Yarrows. She was to take the vessel to Portsmouth Naval Depot, where ammunition would be loaded, and the rest of the crew embarked. A full complement was 55 hands, but right now she was manned by a skeleton crew of just 20. Her first officer was Lieutenant Frank Johnson. The only other officer was the ship's pilot.

The sub had just cleared the Firth of Clyde and was heading out into the open sea. The skipper had just come down the ladder from the Bridge and was scanning her computer screens.

"OK team, here we go," she called. Then loudly, " DIVE THE SUBMARINE ". Frank and the Bridge team came crashing down from above.

The Lieutenant shouted, "All hatches secured, ma'am."

"Periscope depth, helmsman, steady as you go," commanded Paula. The two officers spent the next ten minutes scanning all the gauges, monitoring the crews' reactions.

Once satisfied, Paula looked at Frank, "Well, First Lieutenant, shall we go to the wardroom and complete the handover paperwork?" He nodded his acceptance and as they made their way to the wardroom, she called, "Pilot has the con."

Just a few minutes after settling into the wardroom, came the announcement.

"CAPTAIN TO THE CONTROL ROOM."

The two of them quickly re-entered the control room. Sparks (the radio operator) had picked up a weak S.O.S. signal. He said, "It's about one mile ahead and here's the surprise skipper. It's at one hundred metres."

Frank showed it to her on the electronic charts. "Christ" sighed the skipper, " it's another submarine. It's not supposed to be here." "Also" said Frank, "it's not showing up on the radar or sonar screens." The signal was coming from a point within a section of the chart marked with red shading. They all looked at each other and echoed "Area Z."

"Sparks. Any updates?

"Aye Captain, " he said, "signal is on automatic and getting weaker, and here's the bit you won't like......It's Russian."

"Shit." said Paula, "Russkies in the restricted area. We can't leave sailors like ourselves to a dark watery death."

Paula looked at the sub's position on both the electronic and paper charts. It was right on the edge of the danger zone. To the pilot she said, " How far in are they, pilot?" He replied, "800 metres, ma'am. About half a mile."

Frank said, "Skipper, is the zone that bad? It looks ordinary on the charts. And it isn't even marked on the charts for surface ships, is it? The Navy banned all submarines from going into Area Z. And that is all I know."

"Okay then," said Paula. "We agree it's dangerous in there. We don't know why. And a Russian vessel has got itself caught up in something." She continued. "Right, I'm going to get some guidance from H.Q. Sparks, send a coded message to Faslane. Give our position. Then, Russian naval distress signal detected within Area Z. Please advise."

Sparks quickly complied with her instructions. Then he called out, "Message sent, ma'am." Then a few seconds later he read a reply off his screen from Faslane.

"Only enter Area to rescue possible situation. Mission may be aborted at any time according to Commander Sinclair's understanding of the situation. Will send surface vessels to your location."

Paula thought to herself, "Not a lot of guidance there. Okay, but I've got to take command." Then forcibly she said aloud, "Okay team. We're going in. We are going to make a snatch rescue, then back out the way we came."

To the helm team, "Full speed ahead, steady as you go, maintain present depth."

To one of the technicians, " Yeoman, put the images from the forward-facing cameras on the main screen."

A shout came from the helmsman, "Struggling to maintain this depth, ma'am. She keeps wanting to go down."

Paula and Frank moved over to his position. Sure enough, they could see the depth gauge increase, then the helmsman would steer her back up using the aft planes. Frank quickly scanned all the instruments. "All control surfaces are okay, ma'am. It's like we're getting heavier."

Paula thought to herself, "Is something pulling us down?"

The pilot called out " 100 metres to target, skipper."

Paula felt like she was on one of those simulator courses where they make everything go wrong. She called out," Thank you pilot. Helmsman, tell engine room, slow ahead. Frank, now we're losing way if you control depth with ballast tanks. Pilot, if you stop us 10 metres from target." Paula now focused on the image looming up on the video screen. It looked very strange, some type of mini sub.

It was about 20 metres long, had the traditional tubular submarine shape but kind of flattened out. There was a conning tower but lower and longer than you would expect, with a few portholes on either side. It was probably the only section of the vessel where the crew could stand up. The colour was strange too. Not the usual steel or black shades, more beige coloured.

"I have seen something similar in intelligence reports." said Paula. "Putin told the Navy to build a rescue sub that can go down to a thousand feet, the deepest their subs can go. But Putin likes to deceive and out-manoeuvre people. He used this as an opportunity to start work on a stealth vessel.

His naval engineers were instructed to find a new construction material that won't show up on radar or sonar screens, and a new propulsion system that won't generate any noise. American naval intelligence picked up on this a few years ago. The artist's impressions, the undercover agents sent back, look exactly like that."

She pointed at the screen. "They reported it had some type of jet propulsion system, with liquid being sucked in through those gill-like vents at the front. The hull is made of glass reinforced plastic or carbon fibre. Didn't know it could go to those sorts of depths."

She continued, " See that large round protrusion at the bottom of the craft. Well, that can latch on to the escape hatch of just about any submarine, Russian or otherwise."

"Okay" said Paula, "let's focus on what we do know."

The pilot shouted, "Well there's light emerging from the portholes, so they must have power."

Frank added, "It also seems to be able to maintain its depth, about 10 metres off the bottom. So, some control is being exercised.

That reminded Paula, "how's our depth Frank?"

"We're five metres off the bottom. I'm constantly bleeding air into the ballast tanks to stop us going down into the mud."

Paula thought to herself "Great, possible survivors and not much time to rescue them."

She picked up a radio handset, "Leading Seaman Peterson to the control room."

A few seconds later, a tall burly sailor came through from the forward torpedo room. He was the only qualified diver aboard. Paula knew this super-fit young torpedo technician would be ideal for the job she had in mind. At six feet, he had to squeeze through the control room hatch. When Paula saw him, she waved him over to the video screens. She pointed at the mini sub and said to him, "I've got a tough job for you, Mr. Peterson. Do you think you can handle it?"

"No problem, ma'am, " he replied.

After a short discussion, Peterson headed off to use the escape hatch in the forward torpedo room. Once Peterson struggled through the forward hatch, the Chief Petty Officer came in through the after hatch.

"Issues ma'am," he shouted.

She took a couple of deep breaths and calmly said, "Do tell, Chief, do tell."

He started. "We noticed some of our levers and valves getting stiffer ma'am. So, we stripped them down to oil and greased them. Then discovered they were covered with a light layer of rust. Nothing like this happened on the trials, but anyway, we're removing that rust ma'am."

Paula mused for a few seconds, then replied, "Okay Chief, could you check the other compartments for similar issues and report back to me?"

"Will do, Boss."

Meanwhile, Peterson had now enclosed himself in the escape compartment. Soon it was flooded, and he could open the hatch above him. He swam up through the hatch into the watery world outside. Pressing the transmit button on his radio, he announced to the control room, "I've exited the boat, skipper. Now heading towards mini sub."

Paula watched him on the video screens. Then she asked Frank, "How's the depth situation?"

"Still bleeding air into ballast tanks," he replied. "But she's still descending. Two meters off bottom now." He added, "we're either being pulled down or getting heavier."

Paula replied, "And yet that mini sub just sits there, hovering at ten metres no problem." She mused. "It's made of plastic; we're made of steel." She was interrupted by a voice on the tannoy.

"About to enter mini sub through lower hatch," announced the diver. He was surveying the protrusion all around the hatch. "You're right ma'am. This is designed to rescue other subs. I can see a thick rubber seal around the hatch to make a watertight connection with other subs."

He continued, "Another thing skipper, hatch and all its fittings are not made of steel, they are made of some sort of plastic." They watched him go in through the hatch then close it behind himself. "That's me draining the compartment. I will call back once I'm inside the sub."

"Ok" replied Paula, "keep us informed."

Just then the Chief came back into the control room. "Sorry ma'am. But ALL compartments are starting to build up layers of rust. It's like the sub's aged a few years. I've got technicians derusting everywhere."

"Thanks Chief. Carry on," she said. Paula approached him and whispered in his ear, "Could you focus on the escape hatches, Chief. "

"Understood, ma'am."

"Well team," said Paula, "it looks like our boat is turning in to a rust bucket." "Sparks," she shouted, "any contact with Faslane?"

"No," he replied. "It's like something is blocking our signal. Also, Peterson's signal is getting weaker. I'll try to boost it."

Paula whispered to the Lieutenant, "I'm really close to aborting this mission, Frank."

The tannoy interrupted their conversation. "I'm inside the sub now."

Paula was relieved that Sparks was able to boost Peterson's signals. "Understood, Peterson. How's the atmosphere?"

"My meter says it's ok. Removing my mask now. There are three bodies. I'm at the first one now. He's cold, limbs stiff, no pulse and no breath. Second one now. Just the same ma'am." A few seconds pause. "I'm checking number three now. Yeah, just the same. Sorry skipper, all three are dead. " A silence and a numbness came over the control room.

Paula broke the melancholy. "Peterson, is there any sign as to why they died?"

"Nothing obvious, skipper. The air is ok. No signs of asphyxiation. No signs of trauma. But there is one strange thing boss."

"Continue," said Paula.

"From my diver courses," said Peterson, "I know all our mini sub crews are young fit guys. I'd assume the Russians are the same. But these guys are ancient ma'am. And I mean ancient. To me, they look in their nineties."

"What the hell is going on in this place," thought Paula. "Crew of men......died of old age?"

The tannoy lit up and Peterson's voice came through, "I'm going forward to check out controls."

" So, it looks like something caused the Russians to get old and our boat to get old. And it's pulling us down into the mud." Paula's thoughts continued, " we have got to get out of here." Into the mike she called, "Chief, in ten minutes we will surface the boat."

Frank looked at her. "That's all the ballast tanks blown ma'am. They are empty of seawater and full of air. Yet we are lying on the bottom. We should be shooting up like a cork."
"Have you got plenty of air pressure?" she asked. He nodded.

"My last trick Frank, when I give the order SURFACE, blow out all the diesel fuel in the fuel tanks. Helmsman, you put the forward planes to hard up." Into the mike, "Chief, when I order SURFACE, build the motors up to full speed."
"Aye," he replied.

Again, into the mike, "Peterson, how are you doing over there?" "I think I've got the controls figured out, ma'am." He then started to manoeuvre his craft in all directions. "Yup, no problem, Boss. Plenty of air pressure. Plenty of battery power, and no rust."

"Thank God for that," thought Paula. "Ok Peterson, in a few seconds you're going to see us rising. You follow us up."
"Will do, ma'am. I can see the sub is well down into the mud."
"It's now or never then," thought Paula. She and Frank

looked at each other. Then she ordered into the mike, " all hands, all compartments, stand by to surface."

"SURFACE," boomed Paula.

Sailors busied themselves everywhere. Flicking switches, opening valves, shouting confirmations of their actions. The boat shuddered, jerked, and moved a few inches. Then stopped and silence.

"Try again Chief," she shouted. Another shudder, another jerk, and then another stop. Now she gave the Chief peace. Then came an even more subdued shudder.

The Chief's voice came over the tannoy. "Skipper, I'm checking prop shafts." "Understood chief." Now to Frank, "The fuel tanks?"

He replied, "Fully blown out, full of air, yet no extra buoyancy." "Skipper," called the Quartermaster. "Some switches and warning lights didn't work. I'm going to look at the electronics."

Within seconds he had a control panel stripped. "Boss, look. Diodes, relays, circuit boards. Everything covered in rust." The chief again on the tannoy. "Prop shafts, skipper. Totally caked in rust. Take us 24 hours to free it."

Paula thought, "In 24 hours we will look like those Russian sailors." Into the mike, she ordered, " Forget it Chief, focus on the forward escape hatch." The Chief knew what her next order would be.

"I think it's time for plan B, Frank." She spoke.

He sighed and said " Aye, aye ma'am." He knew what was coming. He knew this would be tough for Paula. But she wasn't shirking from it.

Paula contacted the mini sub now. "Mister Peterson, you will notice we are having some problems. We need a taxi home. Could you clamp on to our forward escape hatch?"

Peterson had been expecting and preparing for this. "No problem, ma'am. That's exactly what this baby was built for. On my way." She watched him start the manoeuvre on the screens, then they pixelated and went blank.

Sparks said, "that's our systems tripping out now, skipper." She nodded back. She tried the address system. That wasn't working either.

Therefore, she went to the control room's forward hatch and shouted, "All hands, control room." Then went to the after hatch and shouted the same order. People started milling into the control room.

Within 30 seconds, 19 people were squashed into the control room. "Okay everyone, listen in," commanded Paula. "As you probably know, our sub is trapped on the bottom. We're 110 metres below the surface. We can't wait for rescue because everything down here ages instantly; metalwork, electrics, even us. So, we're getting out now. The Russian sub we came to rescue, will hopefully rescue us."

They could hear bangs and clanks on the hull. "The noises you can hear, that is mister Peterson clamping onto the forward escape hatch. Take your life jacket and your air supply mask. No personal belongings. Order of battle; the Chief goes up first, then torpedo room staff, then engineering staff, then control room staff. The First Lieutenant will check your name off, as you go into the escape chamber. Chief, could you take the midshipman to help you? Okay team, any questions? (There were none). Let's move forward."

The Chief and his young assistant had finished preparing the forward escape compartment. The compartment was shaped like a vertical tube. About twelve feet tall and three feet in diameter. A slightly inclined ladder led from the bottom to the round escape hatch at the top. At the bottom, access was through an oval shaped hatch doorway. They could hear all the clanking and banging noises had stopped. Now they just needed a signal from Peterson, that it was safe to open the hatch.

The bottom of the mini sub was a similarly shaped compartment. Peterson had the top and bottom hatches open. He checked there were no leaks, now he had to signal the team below. "Hmmm. No radio," he thought. All naval divers had to learn morse code. He grabbed a large valve key and jumped to the bottom of his compartment. Standing on the stricken ship's hull, he banged the hatch with the steel bar, thinking, "I hope some of the guys have brushed up on morse code."

The Chief and the midshipman heard the controlled banging. Then excitedly said together, "Morse code." "But I haven't looked at that for twenty years," said the Chief.

"I have, Chief," said the midshipman. "That's three long thuds. That's O. Long thud, short thud, long thud. That's K." The two looked at each other, then screamed excitedly together.

"OK." "Well done son," said the Chief. "Now let's get up there and open that hatch."

They both hung precariously off the ladder and tried to turn the control wheel. It barely moved. Rust. Peterson could see on his side the rusty wheel hardly moving. He looked at his valve key. He fitted it onto his control wheel, sat down with his back against the bulkhead, and put his feet on the steel bar. He gave a mighty shove with his powerful legs. Just a couple of millimetres at first. Then with a worrying crack, it moved six inches. He threw his valve key to the side and started turning the wheel by hand. Once he had it in the fully open position, all three of them pushed and pulled at the rust covered hatch, till it was in the fully open position.

"Hello Chief" shouted Peterson, "hope my banging didn't wake you up."

The Chief growled back "No, no, son. We just thought you were practicing your parallel parking. Is it all safe up there?"

"Yeah, we are good to go, boss."

The Chief looked downwards and called out, "We are good to go, Lieutenant."

Johnson, at the bottom of the compartment, leaned back through the doorway hatch and shouted off towards the control room, "Vessels clamped together, captain. We now have access to the rescue craft."

Paula sighed with deep regret, looked around, then gave a loud forceful command, "ALL HANDS, ABANDON SHIP." So loud even Peterson in the mini sub could hear it. Now the crew had permission to leave the sub. After a few seconds, she worked her way forward. Meanwhile, in the escape compartments, Peterson had gone back up into the mini sub and stood by its top hatch. The Chief stayed at the joint between the two subs and sent the midshipman up. Peterson helped him through the hatch. At the bottom of the compartments, Frank was shepherding people up the ladders, while he was ticking off their names. After only two minutes, he'd ticked off 19 of the 20 names. "Now the skipper, " he thought. She stepped through the hatch and secured it behind herself. Frank showed her the roll call, as he ticked off the last name, COMMANDER P. SINCLAIR. On the way up she stopped at the bottom of the mini subs compartment and secured the lower hatch.

She shouted upwards, "Bottom hatch closed and secured."

Peterson shouted back, "Aye, aye, ma'am." Now he could start disconnecting the two vessels. She accepted helping hands whisking her through the upper hatch.

As she was lowered down to the deck, she surveyed the alien craft's unfamiliar interior. It was bright, spartan, and most importantly, free of rust. In the forward seats she saw a competent looking Mr Peterson. Down each side of the boat was a row of seats facing in at each other, all filled with familiar faces. Her pensive mood was broken as Frank slammed the hatch shut, securing it with the control wheel, and calling out, "Upper hatch secure."

Time to get back to work. "Unclamping procedures, Mr Peterson?"

"All complete, ma'am.".

The conning tower had a hatch at each end. "Pilot, if you could stand by the after hatch, and, Lieutenant, the forward one." Both officers liked that. It meant they could stand up, hang off the access ladders, and have good views out the portholes. Paula looked round at everyone. "I don't know what sort of reception committee is waiting up top for us. So, stay in your seats, stay calm, stay quiet, and my orders can be heard. If we do have to exit this vessel, keep your life jackets on. I know the hatches are smaller, but you will fit through even with the jacket on. Okay team, are we ready to go home?" There were nods and murmurs of assent everywhere. She turned and addressed her mini sub pilot, "Do you know how to surface this thing, Mr Peterson?"

He replied, "No problem, ma'am."

Then loudly she commanded "MAKE IT SO."

He moved the throttles forward and settled the speed on five knots. Now a slight up angle with the planes. Finally, pumping water out of the ballast tanks with compressed air. When the UP angle got to 10 degrees, he held the controls in that position. Paula noticed her two officers had their scrappy old submariner's caps on. "Pilot, Lieutenant, for recognitions sake, when you open the hatches, keep your caps on."

After only 60 seconds, she noticed a change come over the boat. She looked at Peterson, he was levelling off the boat. The conning tower burst through the surface. Water cascaded everywhere. Daylight streamed in through the portholes. The boat started to rock. The Pilot and the First Lieutenant quickly opened the hatches and climbed up a few steps.

Frank shouted back down, "We've got company, ma'am. Two MTBs (motor torpedo boats) and they're armed to the teeth."

Paula smiled at everyone, "Nothing to worry about. Faslane have sent us a welcome home committee." She wasted no time in swapping positions with Frank.

Either side of them, about 20 metres away, were the large MTBs. Both bristling with machine guns, all pointing at the mini sub. One of the ships cruised up closer to the mini sub. A Lieutenant on the bridge shouted down.

"Commander Sinclair, I presume."

"That's correct," she replied.

"My orders ma'am are to escort you into Faslane. Please maintain radio silence. Keep all radars and sonars turned off. Maintain a course directly behind my vessel, stay about 20 metres astern. The other MTB will stay directly astern of you. Any deviation from these instructions could result in "unpleasantness". Do you understand, Commander?"

Paula said to Frank, "That veiled threat wasn't particularly well veiled."

Then to the MTB officer, "Understood Lieutenant. Please lead on." She called down the hatch, "Did you get all that, Mr Peterson?".

"Every last word, ma'am. I will follow that big grey thing."
"Can you see ok through the forward portholes? " she asked.
He replied, "no problem."

Now her thoughts switched back to her crew. She dropped back down to the deck. Having a good look at everybody she asked if they were all ok.

They all nodded and murmured, "Fine." But she knew there had to be stress and anxiety issues. "Okay everyone, the two vessels you see are Royal Navy torpedo boats. They are here to escort us into Faslane. We are now all super safe. We all need some fresh air and a change of scenery, so every five or ten minutes, pop up and look through the hatches. There are beautiful Scottish hillsides, either side of us. So, relax. Chill out. What do think, Pilot? Three hours to Faslane?"

"Spot on, ma'am," he replied.

"Now, I must check on Peterson."

She went forward and sat next to him, "How are you doing, Mr Peterson? So much of this has landed on your shoulders."

"I'm doing just fine, boss," he replied. "To be honest, I've enjoyed it. Much better than stripping torpedoes down."

"I don't think we could have done it without you. I'll be putting you forward for recommendations. Anything I can do for you right now?"

"No, ma'am. I'm happy right here. Maybe send the helm team forward, and I'll show them how to control the sub."

"Okay," said Paula. "But once they've got the knack, you head up there and take a break," she said pointing to the hatch.

Paula decided to give herself a break. She went aft and settled down next to the Chief. The sailors nearby all shuffled up and gave them some room. "Well Chief," she said, "we'll soon be home."

"And you've brought the whole team home, ma'am. As well as capturing a Russian stealth submarine."

"Chief, it's them that's brought me home." Then, sleepily, "I'm so tired, Chief." But he was already asleep.

Faslane Naval Base, Gare Loch, Scotland

Three hours later, Peterson was manoeuvring the boat into a covered submarine pen in Faslane. As soon as he bumped up against the dock, a shore party secured the vessel and positioned a gangway. Peterson felt the tiredness hit him like a wall. He assumed it was the adrenaline and 'focus' leaving him. So, he allowed himself to fall asleep, draped over the controls. Several minutes later the base commander arrived in a black Range Rover. He marched up the gangway shouting, "Commander Sinclair."

No reply. No one stirred.

He looked at the MTB's Lieutenant inquiringly. "She's definitely in there, Sir." He clambered through the hatch and climbed down the ladder. Looking forward, he saw a sailor asleep at the helm. "I'll have him charged later," he angrily thought to himself. Then his anger turned to shock.

He saw a group of half-dazed people, muttering and moaning. He saw a group of people correctly dressed in naval uniforms. He saw a group of eighty-year-old people.

Partition

by Yasmin Hanif

Refugee trains pass through the mother land.
Carrying loads of closely held heartbeats.
The small, the large, the shaken, and the beat.
Share the same hope, the desire, and the need
To live.

Clutching their golden ticket tighter,
They breathe
A little longer and a lot deeper.
A one-way track to freedom from a divide.
Nation, Religion, and Pride. A divide,
their hearts, souls, and minds
left behind.

The train gets faster, the load becomes heavier.
Speedy, wet eyes make the land blurrier.
The sun grows hotter,
the day becomes wearier.
Then the carriages are set alight.

The land melts away,
with it the blackened ticket.
The train and its contents.

It burns.
People are used as logs.
They burn.
The small, the large, the still, no longer beat.

Except the driver

who departs

the silent tomb

across the Great Divide.

Reflections on Autism
By Megan Peoples

Autism. A word said often yet frequently misunderstood and vilified. When people learn that I have it I'm often asked the following questions. Sometimes out of genuine curiosity, sometimes because they have a loved one with the condition as well and would like to learn more to support them. Just what is it, and how does it affect people?

Let me give you an example, my life.

You were told you were "special" ever since you can remember. That doesn't mean anything since everyone's parents tell them that. Sure, your voice is loud, plus you don't understand some jokes, but that isn't too bad. You are told you are disabled and that you need extra help, but doesn't everyone need a little help every now and then? You know the rules well enough to play tag and that is all your classmates care about. They always come to your birthday parties so you must be friends. Being different isn't bad.

Then you turn twelve.

Suddenly, you start hearing new words in your new school. The big school you move into, away from the safety of the school you spent seven years in. "Retard", "spaz" and "mongo", they shout as you walk from class to class. The children you spent your younger years with are now teens. Teens that want nothing to do with you. Some refuse to respond to you, others called you words you now know to be insulting, although that's mostly thanks to the reactions of the other teens standing by. Being different is bad now. You are no longer you; you are now the class freak. You try to ask for help, but it never comes. It gets worse. They call you a grass and sometimes they throw more than just words. You try one last time to ask for help. Just ignore it, they say. It's hard to do when the words are no longer circling around you but have now infected you within. When you look in the mirror, you see the monster they proclaim you to be.

You understand how you are different now. They call it Autism. You hate it. You hate yourself and try to learn how to fix it. They say it's a disease, so you study to find the cure. If it is a gift like your parents say, then where is the receipt? Why can't you be normal? You lash out at yourself. The temporary physical pain distracts from the inner turmoil.

As you age, you see the world start to change. The label placed on you remains, but the meaning shifts. It is no longer a curse, just a condition. A condition better understood now. You see young children gifted with tools to help them navigate this world better. It warms your heart, but a small part of you is jealous that you were never afforded those. You weren't understood by so many. But you know the next generation will have a better go of it than you and your contemporaries. It fills you with the hope that they will never experience what you had to endure.

Granted, those words still linger. You can hear whispers in the stares you get sometimes when you talk too loudly, too fast and too much. When you fail to make correct eye contact, fail to infer meaning and fail to say the right thing. You are still made to feel shame about something that you cannot change, no matter how hard you try.

In cases like mine, you are referred to as "high functioning", which means you are different enough to be ostracized but not "special" enough to qualify for support. You get well-intentioned praise, which has the unintended effect of highlighting that you are different. Such as "you talk so well for an autistic, you are so brave" and the like. Maybe even comments claiming that you are faking a condition for sympathy or that you shouldn't be working in the field you are.

You still end up making a mess out of nothing sometimes, maybe even landing yourself in a scary situation or two, often fearing physical retribution from those you encounter. It seems whether you stand your ground or hold your tongue, you can still end up in hot water. You are one of the lucky ones, others may have been taken advantage of in worse ways. You hear horror stories from others like you and survive a few yourself.

Progress has been made in the years since my diagnosis, but we aren't out of the woods yet.

I hope my story has given you some insight into what over six thousand Glaswegians experience.

Softplay

by Alan Gillespie

They hit the ballpit

Like a blizzard,

Crashing into plastic pads

In a broth of bony limbs, sticky fingers,

And soft pastel shades.

This World of Wonder, full of

Big bruisers too grown now for the slides,

Weekend dads armycrawling in denim,

Yummy mummies scrolling for likes,

And the occasional grandpa asking

'Where did that wee bugger go?'

Princesses run

Screaming for help

From tigers in turrets.

A little redhead is shouting: 'I'm the shopkeeper!

So, what are you buying?'

At the far table a family of monsters,

Red as beetroot, drink from shimmering cans,

As the volcano spills over.

And the shy girl

In the pale green uniform

(She's got her exams coming up)

Brings out the trays.

There's nuggets for the wee ones,

Chocolate brownies for the old folk,

And strong coffees which neither the mums

Nor the dads

Will ever get round to drinking.

But you never know what might happen.

The Canal

By A J Kennedy

Wildlife

I still keep a dog-eared, black and white snapshot in my wallet of five scrawny-armed four-year-olds in our swimming togs, flopping about in that olive-coated sludge. We imagined we were sailing on Captain Pugwash's "Black Pig." Being the smallest, I was always Tom, the cabin boy.

We surfed belly flops up and down the patchy grass that struggled out of the nearby quarry tip, our vests pea-coloured. Worms, earwigs, and dung beetles plucked from right under the rickety bridge, over the canal populated our hand-patted, damp earth castles.

Whether it be rats, voles, bluebottles, my granddad and Shuggie's Auntie Nellie, the three-legged fox with its amputated tail, my granddad and Jim's Auntie Elsie, or swans, spotting the local wildlife was much more entertaining than being dragged round the zoo.

But the swans were the highlight, the stars of the show, the stately monarchs overseeing our adventures.

Once, I waded through the slush to pick up a newly hatched cygnet. Scum above my waist, my scrawny arms black, I held my hand up with the petrified, peeping creature, and squealed with joy.

'Look, a baby swan.'

Mum shrieked back.

'Tommy, put that back in its…'

With one flick of its wing, the female adult snapped my collar bone.

Still traumatised from being swept away in a flash tide when she was ten, my own mother just gawped, dry mouthed, slack-jawed, blinking. A little girl nudged me safely to the bank.

Mom bought her, the champion of the day, a swan charm bracelet.

That was Hazel. Hazel Mary Morrison.

My first love.

Botany Bound

Despite our best pal, Frankie "Pugwash" Pollock, drowning and dissolving by the paper factory outlet just after his eighth birthday, the four of us, still surviving, snuck up there every weekend.

When the canal was at its peak, bustling trade stretched the old docking area wider and deeper than the rest. We dared each other to shimmy down the stumps of the safety railings, that had long since been sawn off and sold for scrap. But not one of us was daft enough to mess with the silky film floating on the surface.

No matter how sunny it got, the idea of plunging in, never again popped into our heads.

The slum-filled lanes near the docks, where no greenery survived, were still referred to as the Botany. Convicts, bound for a bay of that name in Australia, whined mournful dirges from the prison barges about their last sight of home.

No soul ever made it back.

The Hand of Fate

During our twelfth winter, the poisoned body of lifeless stew froze over. No easy feat, they said on the news. In the backwater beside the crumbling jetty, one tightly fisted hand pointed up with its frozen index finger from under three inches of ice.

Another victim.

All four of us hopped up and down, poking hawthorn twigs at the disembodied limb. Being the youngest, they forced me to clamber down and tap the ice with my heel.

Visions of the wee Pollock boy's acid-stripped skeleton were still sharp in my thoughts. Just to wind me up, Shuggie and Jim kept chanting Frankie's name as they lowered me down. I was bricking it.

But Hazel egged me on. I COULD do it.

I did.

With the steel toecap of my brand-new Doc Martin, I chipped a hole in the ice. Jim and Shuggie held my belt, I held my breath, Hazel held my fate in her hand.

It never occurred to us to call the police. Where was the fun in that? In case the finger came up attached to an arm, or maybe more, our two brave friends shuffled their feet away.

Hazel clung on even tighter.

At the first tug, the accusing finger snapped off. Unlike the great heroes who let go and dived backwards ten yards, she never wavered, until the rest of the air-filled rubber glove slapped her on the cheek. We giggled so much, all four of us ended up kissing.

Local Hero

Adolescence caught us totally unprepared for the changes. Hazel spent more and more time sitting on the bridge with her feet hanging off, smoking and chatting about the facts of life with the older girls.

Just after we turned fifteen, her big brother, Hamish, plunged in to save a little boy.

The ambulance men hosed them both down for twenty minutes before they would touch them. Hamish Morrison turned into quite the local hero, a photo in the papers, on the news, even received a medal from the Lord Provost.

Posthumous, of course. Still, we were all properly chuffed.

The Piano

When Hazel and I snuck into her bedroom for a bit of a cuddle and took in the white space on the wall, her face went whiter than usual, her speech spluttered to a stop, her legs gave way. Mrs Morrison had sold the piano without telling her daughter.

'Mum!'

'It was to pay for you and your wee boyfriend here's joint eighteenth birthday party, sweetheart. You never play it anyway.'

Hazel cried and cried for hours. Through the sobs, I made out only one word.

'Diary. My diary.'

'What diary?'

'I stashed it behind the bass strings.'

When I couldn't stop myself from giggling, Hazel launched into attack mode.

'Laugh? Are you simple? All our secrets; you fat prick. Everything.'

'Hey. Watch your mouth. Don't call me... In fact. You know. I can't take this anymore. You can stick your...'

Hazel yanked out a lock of her hair, whipped me with the bleeding roots and dashed out. In an often-replayed scene, she slammed the door. By the time I caught up, Hazel was already scaling the wall of the bridge.

'I'll jump if you don't go back with me.'

A wild flame of anger lit up her eyes, a fire I hadn't seen before. She meant it. For the first time, a heavy weight tugged down my gut. I offered my hand to Hazel, and she stepped down.

Stupidly, we got back.

The weeks trudged on. She grew more and more desperate for my attention, and her temper flared up quicker and quicker. I could never please her. The constant taunts hit like a hailstorm; stinging and relentless.

My heart seeped from a million pricks.

Seven out of Twenty

One year later to the day, I spotted Hazel's old piano, smashed up on the quarry tip beside the canal. Behind the strings was her journal, sheathed in plastic. I shouldn't have opened it, but I couldn't help myself.

In her precise spidery script, she wrote about me in great detail. Silly, pathetic me, my depressions, my adolescent doubts, my bulimia. In even more eloquent language, she outlined her flings with Shuggie and Jim, according to each a score out of twenty. She gave me a seven.

We stayed motionless on the canal bench, her hands clutching the diary to her chest. She spoke softly, her voice echoing in the stillness of the mid-afternoon.

'I was messing about with different styles like what we're studying at Uni. It's all fiction. Storytelling exercises.'

'Yeah, sure.'

'You know. Virginia Woolfe, Chekov and…'

'It's over, Hazel. I…'

'You're so clueless, chubby, cabin boy. You always have been.'

Once more, Hazel tried the stale, overplayed tottering on the bridge trick, expecting me to cave in.

That time, I let her go for it.

I just managed to duck the acidic mud spattering up. She plunged five feet. The muck only reached her knees. I still remember her startled expression and the red trail of blood where the charm necklace broke and scratched her neck.

I never set eyes on her again.

Full Circle

To mark my fiftieth birthday, I revisited the neighbourhood of my youth. The scarcely recognisable canal was by then harbouring gaudy tourist barges, which glided their way along its winding veins. Next to the modernist, stainless steel bridge, a faceless town councillor unfurled a modest curtain on a plaque to the memory of those lost to the evil waters.

Hazel Mary Morrison was listed third to last.

A high-pitched squeal transported me back forty-odd years. Beyond the plinth, in the newly opened outdoor swimming pool, a little boy was holding up a charm bracelet he scooped up from the bottom.

'Mummy, look. A baby swan.'

'Tommy, put that back.'

More beautiful by the hour
A sonnet by Barney MacFarlane

Those lavish orchids, rare and barred from view,

Since nature strove to keep its prize obscure,

May not match the disarming glance from you:

An eyelid raised ... your fragrant throat ... that lure.

Your qualm, though, is that time will fade and breach

Such gleaming bounty (which makes others dull).

Fluids drained, cracked whispers in your speech

To curse the tyrant rattling in your skull.

Yet, truth be told, that ogre is maligned,

As any swivelling neck will ascertain.

In this bequest, time has been more than kind.

His fortune willed to you, the rest's left plain.

Thus, when your summoned sap pays you no heed,

My hung-jawed sigh is all the proof you need.

The Memory Man

By Hugh V. McLachlan

He sat in his office in the university after the afternoon nap, which now always followed his lunch in the refectory. He pondered. 'There's one in every crew, they say: a moaner.' The elderly gentleman was wondering where he had first come across that saying, if it was a saying. He could not remember. Had he made it up himself? Had he read it? In one of Joseph Conrad's tales, perhaps? He could not remember.

His memory bank, he would often say, was better stocked than it ever had been. However, he would add, the opening hours had become very restrictive and unpredictable. This was said in the tone of a jest, but his quip was provoked by a realisation of mental decay and the fear of a living oblivion.

He was, by nature a gregarious man. He liked conversation and company but had become solitary and lonely. Since his mother died, many years before, he had lived alone. Since his relationship with Florence, a few years before that, there had been no romantic associations of any sort. She died of cancer.

Her illness was in remission when they met and, for some time, she told him nothing about it. She was too embarrassed to tell him that she wore a wig to hide the baldness caused by her medical treatment. Later, when she became aware of the strength of her feelings for him, following the advice of her 'perruquier' – that is, her wig fitter – undauntedly, she removed her wig in front of him.

In a romantic flourish, which was also a sincere expression of a love which was actual, even if only yet in embryonic form, he, in response, took off his shirt to reveal to her the psoriasis on his torso.

In the refectory, when he was having his lunch, he had sat near a small group of people, none of whom he recognised. Who were they? What were they? They were happy to tell him. They were examination invigilators. They were casual, temporary employees of the university. Although they all seemed younger than he was, they were all retired. The few hours they spent were regarded by them as an outing of a sort. It was a change of scene and a chance to make new friends and to meet again fellow invigilators they had met on previous occasions. They were a jolly bunch. The payment they received was, they suggested, almost incidental. They were by no means trying to eke out meagre pensions.

He told them of an experience he had, as an invigilator at a previous university, many years before. He had been appointed there as a senior lecturer when he was in his early thirties. Most senior lecturers were much older than that. In those days, the invigilation was done solely by full time, permanent members of the academic staff. There was a nominated Chief Invigilator, who was always a senior lecturer, in charge. He was the nominated Chief Invigilator on the occasion that he told this group of invigilators about. It was his first ever experience of being one.

The examination session lasted for three hours, and the invigilators were required to muster in the examination room some time before the examination started, to receive their instructions from the Chief Invigilator, about the allocation of the various tasks, they would be required to perform. Various examinations of students on different courses were held at the same time in the large Sport's Hall of the University, which was temporarily requisitioned for the purpose.

'I had a list of the names of my fellow invigilators. There were fourteen of them,' said the elderly gentleman.

'A quick roll call soon established that they had all turned up. I asked them to form themselves into seven pairs, A, B, C, D, E, F and G. I suggested that the person on my extreme left and the person next to her could be pair A and the next two people could be pair B and so on. Then I told them of my plan'.

The central and novel feature of his plan concerned the time that invigilators were required to remain in the examination room. He told them that the presence of every invigilator was required in the first half hour of the examination, when the attendance of each student had to be verified, with reference to their identity cards, and in the last half hour, when the requests from students for additional paper, to complete their answers, were likely to be more frequently and urgently made. For the rest of the time, it was not, in his view, necessary to have the presence of every invigilator in the room. During those two hours, all he asked was that one of each of the pairs was present. It was up to each pair themselves how they arranged this. This would mean that they could all get reasonably generous breaks from the monotony of the undemanding but highly unpopular task of invigilation.

Different pairs were also given responsibilities for distributing to beforehand, and collecting from afterwards, the examination papers of different clusters of students.

The elderly gentleman said:

'When the other invigilators were busily laying out the relevant examination question papers on the appropriate, still vacant rows of desks, prior to the time when the mass of students would be allowed to flood into the hall, I noticed that one of them, a very old, miserable, grumpy looking man was talking to another older looking invigilator while repeatedly, furtively glancing towards me. They both shook their heads. Then, they both nodded their heads.'

'It was very disconcerting. Then, the very old, miserable and grumpy looking man seemed to try to sprint off towards another invigilator, and then he grimaced and slowed down his pace considerably. When he reached this other invigilator, he spoke to him, while glancing furtively towards me. They both shook their heads. Then, they both nodded their heads.'

'I was beginning to feel paranoid. When the old man started to walk away from the other invigilator, I had the dreadful suspicion that he was heading for me, and that his clumsy, painful-looking shuffle would soon bring us face to face, if he did not trip and fall, before he reached me.'

'I stood my ground and waited. I muttered to myself: "There's one in every crew, they say: a moaner".'

'When he reached me, he said "Excuse me. About your plan. It isn't really fair".'

"Not fair to whom?", I snarled.

"Not fair to you", he said. "Not fair to you. Your plan gives everyone a break apart from you."

"However," he said, "if it is all right with you, my friend and I have arranged a slight modification of your plan. There must be a Chief Invigilator, who must be a senior lecturer, present at all times. My friend and I are senior lecturers. We have changed the pairings so that we are now in the same pair. There will always be one of us here who can be your deputy Chief Invigilator. You can have a break anytime that suits you."

The elderly gentleman said to the temporary invigilators, who listened attentively to his tale: 'I was truly humbled. He was a better person than I imagined. He was a better one than I was. If there was a moaner in that crew, it was me'.

He enjoyed the short time he spent in conversation with them. He was jealous of them. He simultaneously dreaded and longed for his own retirement.

On the one hand, almost all the many friends and acquaintances he had, worked at the university. Who would he meet, who would he talk to if he retired? What would he do?

Would he read novels again as he used to love to do? Joseph Conrad was the favourite amongst his most favourite authors, yet he had not read anything by him for years, not even his short stories, which he used to love, even more than his novels, and to read and re-read voraciously. The strain of marking so many students' assignments had tended to deprive him of the pleasure of reading for its own sake. However, the main problem was his failing memory.

He had, too, long since stopped doing crosswords. They more and more had taken too long to complete, on the fewer and fewer occasions when he completed them. The words which he groped for had become elusive. They stubbornly evaded his grasp. What had once been an exquisite pleasure became a tedious, frustrating and humiliating chore.

Could he afford to retire yet? Were his savings sufficient? He could not for long feel sure that he could and that they were. He was tormented by the theory of power of the political philosopher Thomas Hobbes, which he did not completely believe but which he could not completely reject either.

Hobbes said that a person's power 'is his present means, to obtain some future apparent good'. Hobbes argued that a person cannot have too much power: we cannot predict the nature and extent of our future needs or wants, hence we can never be justifiably sure, that what we have now, will be sufficient to meet them. The elderly gentleman thought that this well describes the function of wealth. To have money is to have now the means, to meet potential future needs. We can never be sure that we have enough now because we cannot know now what we might need or want in the future, and what might be available, at a price, to meet such needs or wants. People who think they have enough money probably lack both money and imagination. So, he suspected. You can be justifiably sure, that you have sufficient funds for the future, only if you can be justifiably sure, you have very little future. So, he feared.

Yet, on the other hand, the prospect of retirement was in many respects very attractive. He was growing weary. He was unable to do his job, as well as he used to do it. He was struggling to do his job, as well as his own self-respect required him to do it. To deliver lectures, which had for many years been a great pleasure to him, was becoming burdensome and stressful, as it had been for him, at the very start of his career. It would be better to volunteer to leave, before he was forced to do so.

But he had not quite reached that stage yet. Had he? He had been given more lectures to deliver, more classes to take, and more marking to do in recent years. Was this done because they knew that he was still good enough at his job and still popular with the students? Was it done to pressurise him into leaving because he was no longer either of these things?

He sat at his desk, priming himself to re-commence marking the pile of assignments he was working on, before his lunch in the refectory and his postprandial nap in his office. He recalled the first lectures that he ever delivered.

He had been given the opportunity to give a few lectures, one a week for three months, many decades before. Initially, they were dreadful. He seriously thought of giving up. He prepared his early lectures very thoroughly. He was very worried that he would dry up when he was standing in front of the students. He feared that he would forget what he wanted to say. Hence, he wrote down his lectures, word for word. He wrote them down as if they were exemplary essays and recited them *verbatim*. He was distressed to realise that they were, somehow, falling very flat, so he spent even more time and effort in the writing of them.

The lectures were held on Thursdays at 1 pm. He spent much of Mondays and Tuesdays reading, making notes, and thinking about what he would say, and much of Wednesdays writing and polishing the prose of his Thursday lecture. On one of the weeks, he was told in the late afternoon of the Tuesday that Thursday's lecture would have to be postponed that week. He was delighted. He would not have to write a lecture that week. However, on the Thursday, he got a phone call around 12.30 pm, to tell him that there had been a bureaucratic error of some sort, and that his students would be turning up as usual at 1 pm, and that they would be expecting a lecture from him.

He did not have time to write a lecture. All he could possibly do was, to think of what the central points were that he wanted to make in his lecture and write down headings on a sheet of paper, to remind him, what these points were. He started his lecture by telling the students what the points were that he wanted to make in the lectures. Then, he made the points. He concluded his lecture by reminding his students what the points were that he had made in his lecture. He looked at his students, as he delivered his lecture, rather than at sheets of paper, on which his lecture was written. He engaged with them. He looked them in the eye. They looked him in the eye. The lecture was the best he had ever given, the only good one he had ever given. It went down very well. He enjoyed giving it. The students enjoyed listening to it.

When you know what you want to say, what points you want to make, the appropriate words will automatically come to mind. If you focus fretfully on the particular words and wording you will use, the points will get lost. It is the points, not the words that are crucial. Lectures and recitations are different things. These were the lessons he took from that experience. For the rest of his career, they were the principles he acted upon when lecturing. He never again wrote his lectures down beforehand word for word. He never used anything but the flimsiest of notes, mere headings, to remind him of the points he wanted to make.

However, nowadays, when he was lecturing, the words did not always come, even when he was aware of the points he wanted to make. Sometimes, too, he forgot what these points were. The headings on his sheets of paper were often now of no help to him. Yet, he could not revert to writing down his lectures word for word. He would rather retire than do that. He would rather die than do that.

He thought of the terrible time when he took his shirt off after Florence had taken off her wig. She looked at him aghast. He fumbled with his shirt as he tried to put it on again. The buttons seemed so large and the buttonholes so small. There was a dreadful, embarrassed silence before Florence offered the explanation that she was startled by the sight of the crucifix he was wearing and not at all by his blemished skin. She did not realise, she said, that he was a Roman Catholic.

'I am only nominally a Catholic' he said 'But I am not a believer. It's the crucifix my mother wore.'

'I didn't realise that you are a bigoted Protestant' he added.

She smiled broadly. 'It's all right. I'm an atheist', she said. 'We are both atheists. It's all right'.

But it was not all right. He did not believe her. He could not accept, even if he wanted to, that she was not repelled by his psoriasis. He strongly felt that she had been.

Moreover, they were not both atheists. He was not a believer, but he was not a disbeliever either. Scepticism about both the existence and non-existence of God was his position. He had equal contempt for both fervent, dogmatic, proselytising atheists and fervent, dogmatic, proselytising theists. He was horrified by the thought that she was horrified that he was wearing a crucifix as a symbol of religious affiliation.

They met only a few times after that.

The next woman who saw his naked torso was an undertaker.

You are Loved

by Annie Healy

I'm telling you I love you I say as you look back at me unsure

I'm telling you, you are beautiful, no I am not you shout and this is what I must endure

I'm telling you; you are intelligent and witty and good fun to have around

I'm telling you to look up and stop staring at the ground

I'm telling you, you are feminine and a worthwhile human being

I'm telling you as I look into your sad eyes all the beautiful things I am seeing

I'm telling you to stop being a punchbag to release someone else's anger, no self-worth, no self-esteem, no personality left just clothes draped over a skeleton hanger

You are your own worst enemy, you are destroying yourself with deep intention

I'm telling you, you are loved by me

My beautiful awe-inspiring reflection.

HOGMANAY

By Deborah Portilla

Hogmanay just isn't the same these days. If it wasn't for the reruns of Scotch and Wry and Jackie Bird counting down to midnight, would we even know that it was the last day of the year? Everything sounds too civilised on the streets of Southside Glasgow. Could be any normal Friday night. But it's not, it's Hogmanay. Barely a whiff of a party the week before. People just can't be bothered going into town with all the queues and the hassle of getting home. It's all terribly low key these days. It wasn't always like that.

I remember the years I spent living in Castlemilk in the 60s. The new housing estate was built in 1958 to accommodate over 30,000 people from overcrowded areas such as the Gorbals. The houses were a big improvement on previous living conditions and tenants were, on the whole, happy with their lot. We moved into Machrie Road in 1965 and what a friendly neighbourhood it was.

Back then, the streets were jumping with kids. Playing football, just plain old bouncing balls on the back walls, there was always someone out to play. In the heady days of the Scottish summer, we would buy chalk and draw tennis courts on the main road, inspired by a few weeks of Wimbledon on council tv.

Come the end of the year, though it was a different story. The week leading up to Hogmanay would be spent with hours of industrial style cleaning. Every nook and cranny would be wiped down. Every cobweb would be gone. You could eat your dinner from the kitchen floor, so they said. The cooking would start the week before too. My gran would cook a dumpling a few days beforehand. No microwaves or air fryers to speed up the process then. The other thing my gran would make would be tongue. A great big pot of boiling tongue. While not great to look at, once it's cooked and served, it makes the best sandwich filler with chutney. The only time we see tongue now is in sealed packs in Marks and Spencer's though apparently any good butcher will be able to source one for you.

The table would be set by 10 and hell mend us if we took an early bite. There would be enough to feed us for the week. We would wait patiently till the bells then wipe a tear from our eyes as we said goodbye to the previous year and welcomed in the new. The neighbours would wait a civilised 15 minutes and then the doors would start to open and close. Everyone left their door open so that anyone could just walk right in. We would all congregate at my gran's, partake of her fine spread and then move next door to Cathie's. An hour later, we would end up at Mrs. McDonald's on the ground floor and there the party would stay till the wee small hours. Songs would be sung, drinks would flow, and we would do the very same the next Hogmanay. One singer, one song. Those were the days…….

close

by Sean McGarvey

there are sights as a walk down

the bentinck street close

that a wish to live in

harsh cast shadows, bright bold brick

all in red shimmers, red tones

shadows blush

bricks become rubies

ruppled as a see through

glass pane brings new plane, ether

becomings to the light

to tenements, to this back alley

and tae me!

a think of things a wish to spend time with

these sights are one

"paint them and you can spend hooouuurrrss with them"

a n o t h e r t h i n g

as beautiful as that sounds

let it go

it's a wish, a living fairy

let it go

let it go with a wish

let it live with a kiss

a beautiful thought

embedded now, in blue ink, black text

in unheard of Glasgow heat, of west end step

on a page, a book, that a write

my life into, things a wish

things to let go and

things to live in

More than a battlefield
By Samantha Booth

Walking through Battlefield on a summer's evening is always a journey for the senses. The tenement windows open wide with curtains stirring in the breeze. TVs mumble inanely from within, while smells of spag bog, curry or maybe frozen dinner tease the empty stomach. Children squeal with delight as they run in and out of closes and gardens, or maybe through the leafy bounty of Queen's Park. Dogs sniff happily at post boxes as cars pull into one of the coveted spaces as grateful workers arrive home. The 4A bus trundles through the streets, the new electric engines no longer choking the narrow corridors with exhaust fumes or assaulting the ears with the noise of a gruff diesel engines. Mrs Willoughby from Flat 2 of Number 36 though rather misses the sound – it gave her fair warning that it wasn't safe to cross. She consoles herself that apparently these electric buses are saving the Planet so she must make do and just take extra care.

People stride alongside the River Cart on its gregarious journey after one of the many torrential Glasgow showers, perhaps going for an ice cream or to buy a fish supper. Others find their ways to yoga at Langside Halls, while there are those who just want a cool beer in one of the pocket-sized gardens belonging to the bottom floor flats. Or maybe it's to Battlefield Rest, the cosy, rustic Italian restaurant in what was once a tram station described as the most 'exotic tram shelter in Scotland'. And for me that's where the journey of another kind begins.

The summer sky darkens to flat grey nothingness and before me I see steel rails running along the streets, hear the 'ting ting' of the approaching tram and see men in brown jackets and bunnets leaping from back platforms, cigarettes held tight between dry lips. Women in long coats and even longer skirts huddle beneath damp wool to try and escape the biting wind, bags of shopping clutched to their sides or perhaps a brown bag of grapes held trapped between elbow and waist in anticipation of sitting on the bedside cabinet of a patient in the looming Victorian megalith known as the Victoria Hospital. The grey stone encases much misery but also bellies the dry Glasgow laughter that comes from within.

The tenements now are blackened too from the soot of the city that surrounds it, gone is the burnished glow, sparkling windows, and bright breezy curtains of modern days, now the tenements huddle round the streets like men in battered coats, queuing for work. The doors are painted dark and chipped, the tiles in the closes, shades of darkest greens which, when adorned by the inky soulless concrete of the steps and deep burnished wood of the banister, give the feeling of being beneath the deepest murkiest sea. Unless of course, the lamps were lit and then those cavernous closes became magical places of strange happenings, where mysterious beings lurk beyond the dancing flames. Regardless, women of all ages wash those closes day in and day out, year after year, scrubbing and sweeping until they are clean enough to eat a feast of Mother's Pride and jam from.

The middens were a different story. The bins and outhouses in the back were the lands of adventure for the dirty faced children in their clumpy shoes and short trousers, whatever the weather. They might have played at being medieval knights, hammering at each other with broom handles for swords and bin lids as shields. Ironic given that, as I continue to walk, the weather changes again and I am soon surrounded by hawthorn trees in full bloom, their white flowers stark against the pale blue of a spring sky.

It is 1568 and the tenements have vanished in the mist of future times, and I am surrounded by men on all sides amid the few stone and thatched buildings of what was then the village of Langside.

I am lost in the melee where Scot killed Scot over, when it boiled down to it, religion. Some things don't change, but the Battlefield that I see now well deserves that name and is as different to the later editions than could possibly be imagined. Mary's troops have been forced to file through the narrow street of the village, corralled by the hedgerows and gardens, where Moray's men are waiting to ambush them. Acrid smoke leaves little air to breath, explosions are frequent and loud but not even those pyrotechnic bangs can muffle the sound of men killing men, death comes in ugly red washed flurries of clumsy strokes and bursts of desperate strength as men wield oversized claymores and pikes, muskets and pistols. It lasted all of 45 minutes, but the land drank deep of blood that night. Not that you would have caught sight of Mary in person. The former Queen - she had abdicated the year before - having hoped to avoid a battle as she tried to reach the safety of her loyal stronghold at Dumbarton, had stopped to watch from Court Knowe in Cathcart, a place that gave her a full view of the battlefield. It was from here that she fled in defeat, while the ordinary folk of Langside did their best to tend the wounded, bury the dead, calm the horses and right their garden fences.

It wasn't the last blood shed on the route of the 4A bus and nor was it the first. Who knows for sure what other lives have been lost. As I walk through the leafy oasis of Queen's Park the skies shift once more, followed by a distinct shiver as I feel the snow around my feet and flakes, stinging my cheeks in their angry flurries. The orderliness of a park has vanished, and the trees now draw up around me in a way that lets me know they are in charge – we will grow where we will, as high as we please, as broad as we like they seem to say as their stark branches reach out to each other above my head.

Animals watch me warily from the protection of their boughs and trunks, I never quite see them in their glorious entirety, but catch a glimpse here and a glimpse there – a fox perhaps, maybe a badger, possibly a deer. And was that a wolf? A distant howl answers me, but it is not the wild creatures I am here to see. It is the sight before me as I emerge into a clearing that I have slipped back in time to find.

Two men dance before me, one raw and wild with lime stoned hair and dirty checked breeks tied to his legs, the other clean and bristling with olive skin and dark sleek hair, his golden breastplate still managing to catch the light despite the gloom. The wild looking one carries a long, heavy sword while the polished looking one carries a much shorter counterpart and a long, rectangular shield. They thrust and parry, slip and slide, fall and stumble, neither one gaining the advantage as the snow slips from their foreheads and their knuckle's turn blue from the cold. Eventually with unspoken consent they both slump to the ground, too exhausted to kill and too tired to hate. What is the point? Beneath the shimmering breastplate and the lime stoned hair we are the same flesh and blood. Joining hands, they help each other to sit on a fallen tree and lean against each other breathing heavily.

I move on and continue to walk through the ancient woodlands as winter turns to spring, spring to summer and as the leaves start to crispen as I walk beneath their golden offerings to find a cave deep in the land. The deep mossy mouth resting between the roots of two giant oaks is calling out an invitation that I can't resist. In the small round cavern, I find an old woman, sitting on a pile of moss and foliage, beside a small but sprightly fire with a kettle rattling its readiness from a hook above. She smiles and nods and gestures for me to sit. Her face is ancient and as craggy as the land and I find myself wondering if I have come back in time at all, or perhaps this is me returning home to where I belong. I sigh as I take a sip of the hot tea from a clay beaker.

Yes, it certainly feels like this is how it is meant to be, the tenements and the buses, the rushing and the squealing all now seem like an unlikely dream. Here in the stillness of the forest, in the simplicity of a hot cup of tea and a warming fire, is where I belong. And then the sounds of the laughing and playing, the running and the rushing, the buses and lorries encompass me once more and I am stood outside Battlefield Rest wondering if I have time for a quick glass of wine and plate of pasta before I visit the library.

The Waiting Rom

by Jonathan Aitken

I feel your semblance
I see the I
I wonder when the time went by
Bloomed and perished being one
gasping blue the silent sun
Bottled up - a bottleneck
red the colour, stop the cheque,
checkerboard - a flaming lance,
illuminate the darkness - fast
We talked in hum - vibrations last
silence watched you miss the chance,
Chance? the mirror never lies,
stop, but wait - I close my eyes,
Reawaken bright as day,
a foolish thought, a dismal play,
a rope that's tangled holds some strength,
a single strand, but at what length?
I thread myself, I built the web
forgive the spider, quash the debt
I ramble on and on and on,
You touched my face and let me yawn.

Stuck In the Middle
By Bill Brown

Michael had it - "middle child syndrome" - it just hadn't been invented yet. He was the fourth child of a family of seven children born to James and Martha. He used to think of his big sister Ellen as his mini mum because the real Mum was so busy maintaining the household chores, while his dad was this bloke who used to leave for work in the morning before he woke up and came home, just before he was put to bed. Ellen looked after him as his parents seemed to concentrate their love and affection for the eldest sibling, who was very clever and the youngest sibling, who always seemed to be unwell.

It wasn't an unhappy existence. He was always fed, watered, and kept clean. He always had plenty of company, although he often got lost in the melee that was Sunday night, family card night in their household. It was there he met up with numerous cousins and grandparents who also seemed to reserve their interest for the eldest and youngest brothers. He wasn't in the least jealous-too busy getting on with his own life-but he did notice and, often enough, felt anonymous, just a face in the crowd.

Michael attended St Bernard's Primary School in his tiny village cum scheme in Cumbernauld. He had a sibling in nearly every class. The school had a wide catchment area and kids came from Croy, Kilsyth, Stepps and other North Lanarkshire villages cum schemes, which were being thrown up at this time. There were 47 other pupils in the class. Michael Haggerty was the 24th name on the class register, right in the middle. He was not particularly academic, nor was he pushed to be by anyone. His teacher struggled with the kids who were struggling to cope with learning, while his parents focused on fostering their own child prodigy at home.

He was left to his own devices. Michael was quite happy just playing football with the lads in his class. He just did enough work to get by without drawing attention to himself. He would probably qualify for senior secondary had he not contracted jaundice and, consequently, missed his 11 plus exams. He wasn't bothered. He carried on to secondary school in non-academic subjects and followed the trend of his peers. He was destined for an apprenticeship.

Michael sallied on. He started work in his local garage and trained for 4 years as a Motor Mechanic. At first, he was quite satisfied and happy, however, as the time wore on, he began to detest being a grease monkey. He was constantly manky and grubby. He enjoyed the day release classes at college, but he was frustrated by the fact his elder brother had progressed into teaching and his big sister worked in a bank. He saw them in nice clean jobs which did not involve dirt, grime and sweat. He wanted that too. He regretted not working hard enough at school. He wanted a life like that too and decided he would return to education and try to attain some qualifications. He resolved he would serve out his apprenticeship but was determined to go onto to better things. He just didn't know what.

Due to his newfound ambition, much to his parents' surprise, Michael left his job and started to study for O' grades, then Highers at Langside College in Glasgow. He loved the student life and discovered that he had no little ability. He gained sufficient grades to enable him to apply for any course in university. He decided to be really bold. He chose medicine. He did not know what branch of medicine, so he chose to study to become a General Practitioner. There was an added bonus to his appearance at the college. When he was there, he met Chrissie, a girl who worked in a famous Glasgow lawyer's office and was studying Shorthand Typing. He was, for the first time in his life, besotted. She appeared to reciprocate. They had to be patient though because the course he was on took 5 years, a lot of study and life living on a student grant. They both remained living with their parents, which was quite unusual in those days, as they were both in their mid to late twenties and still unmarried. It was much to his parents' pride that Michael graduated as a doctor.

He applied for a job in his local village where he had been raised. He quickly proposed to Chrissie, who had been his sweetheart during all the years of study. She had waited for him. Michael enjoyed and flourished in his new career. He and his wife had 3 children of their own. As was the norm, in those days, Chrissie was a stay-at-home Mum, but Michael employed her as his Secretary/Receptionist. Chrissie never got a minute's peace. If she wasn't running the Mum and Toddlers group with a girl in the village who had children of a similar age, she was answering the phone to Michael's patients. Remember, this was the days before mobile phone and regular hours for GP'S. Very often they would be awoken at 3 am by someone complaining about an itch caused by Athlete's foot or a patient with a wind issue.

However, Michael enjoyed his career and became very well known in the village, which was now a small town. He was there at every crucial moment in the life or death of his patients. He witnessed births, cures, diagnosis, and death for many people as well as the many societal changes. He may have started life as an invisible man but by the end of his career he was a valuable and respected member of the community for his loyal and efficient service. He was regarded as a local hero - a down-to-earth doctor who understood problems and actually cared for his patients.

When he finally retired at the age of seventy, his peers and family arranged a celebration party to commemorate the occasion. Michael was overwhelmed by the list of guests and dignitaries who turned up to wish him well. He gave an impromptu speech to the throng:

"Well! Everybody here, thank you for your support and help over the years. I must say, I had no idea I was held in such high esteem but there you go. A wee lad from a scheme making it to the status of a doctor. Such is the state of our society, and the balls-up our politicians have made of our world, I don't know if it could happen now. Anyway, I will finish on a lighter note, with a small anecdote of one of my first ever house calls.

"It was one day after surgery, I was called out to visit an old lady in Croy, a rundown, ex-mining village. When I arrived, I looked round at the squalor which was evident in the street -abandoned prams, litter, needles, all sorts. I went into the house. It was manky, absolutely filthy. The whole family was there in attendance. The granny who was ill, the Mum and Dad and at least nine children, all doing different activities including fighting and squabbling over games-very noisy. The Mum showed me into the room where the patient was lying in the bed, gasping for breath. I examined her and could see she had a serious chest infection -no surprise given the lack of heating and ventilation. I wrote a prescription to be taken to the pharmacist. I thought, I needed to get out quickly. The stench was making me wretch. The next thing that happened was when I went into the living room and there was a dog there. It defecated on the floor, but nobody reacted or went to clean it up. I couldn't just leave it so I said, " It really is very unhygienic to leave dogshit on the floor like that, especially when the old lady is so ill. You should really clean it up."

The Dad then turned round to me and said " That's not our dog. We thought it was yours. It came in the door with you!" It turned out it was a stray dog who had just followed me through the open door. That was my introduction to life as a GP in a deprived area.

"All I would say to all of you is never let yourself be the insignificant and invisible member of your family or community. We all have talents to share, and it doesn't matter at what age you discover them. You don't have to be an overnight success-just always think your best days are still to come, like I do.

It has been a pleasure to serve you all in this community".
The man in the middle received another well-earned round of applause.

Poppies

by Erin Jamieson

fields of endless poppies:

ivory, violet, velvety red

lush colours erase shadows

and make my body feel whole

as I've longed dreary winter nights

until the startling burst of spring

these blooms may end me

yet they call to me with majesty

my words are inadequate

perhaps, I've always worried

I am inadequate

to belong to this world

of colours and endless

wonder

One Bite of Me

By Jane Jay Morrison

O, I am the ugliest cucumber in the patch!

The others mock me in my loathsome, putrid corpulence, safe in the knowledge they themselves are slender as swan-necks. They are right. I disgust me utterly. In places, my skin is burnished faultless green just like theirs – but elsewhere, it is streaked a pestilent, messy almost-black. O, I despair! My malformations are beyond repair.

My flavour should be clean and crisp as a grasshopper's music; should taste of summers. I should delight tongues in salads, should grace limpid cocktails, and shine as (with the crusts cut off, please) the subtle star of the perfect English afternoon tea. And yet instead, this vile, candy-fleshy putrescence pervades me. I know my taste is only sweated sugar, a mouthful of pink rot and filth-perfumed juice. I have always been the worst of us. I have always grown this way, even though we were but seeds. Upon me the fruit-flies cluster filthily, heralds of my ultimate inner repugnance - whilst they ignore the other cucumbers in the patch.

I know my flesh ought to be the most delicate of greens, the microcosmic elegance of my interior traced through with tiny, translucent, teardrop-pale seeds. But I have no such grace. My seeds crawl at my black heart, vile and beetle-dark in their crunching carapaces.

The children are haring up the garden for a harvest now. I have failed them. I ought to nourish, ought to hydrate, but I cannot even offer them the least goodness. Discard me. Compost me. Trample me underfoot! I am come to nothing, or less. For I am so irredeemably repugnant that one bite of me - I am sure - would simply poison them all. Here they come, here they come…!

"Look!" cried the children, "A lovely watermelon!"

Meet the Contributors

Marco Giannasi transformed a dilapidated former tram halt into the Battlefield Rest, a very popular Italian eatery. He is co-author of Dining Tales, the remarkable stories behind some of Glasgow's most iconic restaurants, to be published in 2024.

Hugh V McLachlan is an emeritus professor of Applied Philosophy and has published several books. He is a renowned authority on the history of witchcraft in Scotland and continues to contribute articles for newspapers and online newscasts as well as appearances on television and radio.

Frank Chambers is the author of crime novels, Lost on Main Street and The Busker of Buenos Aires. He is one half of music duo Kandella, who have released two albums, Flying High and Are You Listening.

Alex Meikle has been CEO of several third sector social care organisations and still provides a consultancy on social care and community-based issues. He is the author of Deception Road and Caledonia Smack and co-author of Dining Tales to be published in 2024.

Henry Buchanan has published several works, including interpretations of Dostoevsky's Crime and Punishment and Shakespeare's A Midsummer Night's Dream. He has also published reviews in literary journals.

Palma McKeown is Scots-Italian and has been published in various poetry magazines and anthologies. She has long been a fan of vintage and now has three stores on Etsy: Blithe Spirit Vintage, Luckenbooth Vintage and Kingfisher Vintage UK.

Jonathan Aitken grew up in the south side and was educated at Hutchesons' Grammar School. He has been working with still and moving images for most of his life. His poetic works explore philosophical, divine and occult themes.

Duncan McDonald is a retired environmental technician. In a previous life he worked in naval shipyards, maintaining an interest in all things nautical ever since. Strange things happen at sea and Duncan loves to write about them.

Lizzie Allan is a graduate of Glasgow University and former secondary school teacher. She writes short stories in various genres and also writes poetry – often with a touch of humour. She enjoys painting, crafting and plays in a ukulele band.

Samantha Booth is a former journalist who has recently published her first novel - The Many Deaths of Aurora Flowers about a woman who can remember her past lives. Now Head of PR for a UK charity, she lives on the south side of Glasgow with her partner, Martin.

Greg Shearer is a working-class Glaswegian poet and spoken word artist. Greg uses his poetry to document and excise the trauma of youth, growing up below the poverty line in a broken home and to expose misrepresented proletarian experience. His work is described as raw, poignant and woundingly accurate.

William Brown started writing personalised tribute poems for family and friends, developed via creative writing groups, U3A and classes. The end product was a book of short stories with a Glaswegian theme called " Twice Last Night". He is now writing novellas.

Alan Gillespie is an English teacher in Glasgow. His debut novel, The Mash House, was shortlisted for the New Dagger Award by the Crime Writers' Association.

Maureen Myant has lived in Battlefield most of her life. She is the author of three published novels, The Search, The Confession and The Deception and a number of short stories. She is working on her fourth novel.

Yasmin Hanif is a Scottish writer and educator, specialising in children's literature. Her first poem was published by Cranachan Publishing in their Stay-at-Home anthology. She has had 8 stories published and an upcoming graphic novel for the 'We Can Be Heroes' project at St. Albert's, where she was also a writer-in-residence. Twitter/X account: @YHanifWrites

Ian Goudie is a former defence worker who has contributed to numerous defence-related publications. Since retiring, he has had a play staged, and several poems and pieces of fiction published. He has an MSc in Public Policy and is currently studying for a BA in Arts and Humanities.

Erin Jamieson (she/her) holds an MFA in Creative Writing from Miami University. She is the author of a poetry collection (*Clothesline*, 2023) and four poetry chapbooks. Her latest poetry chapbook, *Fairytales,* was published by Bottle Cap Press. Her debut novel, *Sky of Ashes, Land of Dreams,* will be published by Type Eighteen Books (November 2023).

Kathryn Metcalfe is a poet from Paisley who is published online and in print, she is one of the Mill Girl Poets, a group of women who wrote and performed a show about the heritage and lives of Paisley thread mill workers. In 2014 she founded Nights at the Round Table, a monthly open mic to showcase writers and poets which still runs nine years later.

Colette Coen was born and bred in Cathcart and now lives in East Renfrewshire where she runs Beech Editorial Services. Recently she has been published in *Five Glasgow Stories* and *Postbox*. Her collection of short stories *Forgotten Dreams* is available on Amazon.
.http://colettecoen.wordpress.com

Bill (Barney) MacFarlane is an ex-journo, having worked on several newspapers, including the Daily Record, Daily Express, Sunday Mail, Sunday Standard, Evening Express in Scotland – as well as stints in Fleet Street and the Home Counties. He has mostly been in editing positions but also wrote columns on the arts.
https://www.thenational.scot/news/15029340.the-scot-who-cracked-the-morse-code/

Deborah Portilla Born and lives Southside Glasgow. Retired 2021 after 41 years in banking. Signed up for creative writing courses and writes about family life and times that have become cherished memories. Enjoys travelling. Favourite places are Italy and NYC where she hopes to find further inspiration.

Sean McGarvey writes to connect to themselves, others, places around them and the world. Sean likes writing formulaic and with freedom. Sean enjoys situating writings where Sean is. Sean finds that they continue writings that may have started years ago which is pleasing. Sean has consistently journalled for 13 years. seanmcgarvey95@gmail.com .

Annie Healy was born & bred in Glasgow to Irish immigrant parents, Annie has written poetry and stories from a very young age, her first fictional book "The Note" will be published and available late 2023/2024. Annie performs regularly on stage portraying strong women but in comedic roles. Life is not always about the right thing, the right choice, the right turn. Try left.

Pratibha Castle is widely published in journals and anthologies including *Agenda, Spelt, Tears In The Fence, London Grip, Orbis, One Hand Clapping, High Window, Fly on the Wall Press,* and forthcoming in *Stand*. Short and longlisted, highly commended and given special mention in numerous competitions, her award-winning debut pamphlet *A Triptych of Birds & A Few Loose Feathers* (Hedgehog Press 2022) is joined by *Miniskirts in The Wasteland* (Hedgehog Poetry Press 2023), a Poetry Book Society Winter Selection 2023.

.

Also from Battlefield Writers

Tales from the Battlefield

More information at
www.battlefieldwriters.com

Printed in Great Britain
by Amazon